Copyright © 2024 by Theophilus Monroe.

All rights reserved. Printed in the United States of America. No part of this book may be used or reproduced in any manner whatsoever without written permission except in the case of brief quotations embodied in critical articles or reviews.

Cover Design by Christian Bentulan: https://coversbychristian.com/

Proofreading/Editing by Mel: https://getproofreader.co.uk/

This book is a work of fiction. Names, characters, businesses, organizations, places, events and incidents either are the product of the author's imagination or are used fictitiously. Any resemblance to actual persons, living or dead, events, or locales is entirely coincidental.

For information:

www.theophilusmonroe.com

MERLIN'S MANTLE

DRUID DETECTIVE AGENCY
THEOPHILUS MONROE

Contents

Part I	1
1. Shadows at the Shire	3
2. Charcoal Prophecies	15
3. Poop Emoji	23
4. Don't be a Karen	37
5. Reasonable Doubt	45
6. A Detective's Dilemma	57
7. Butt Heads in Suits	67
8. Lithomancy	83
9. Custard's Last Stand	95
INTERLUDES I	103
I.1.1. Merlin	105
I.2.3. Sloane	111

PART II 117

10. The Naked Truth 119
11. Tainted Proof 133
12. Hold your Tongue, Say Apple. 145
13. Dicks and Daggers 155
14. ReesesPiscis 163
15. Hell or High Water 173

INTERLUDES II 189

I.2.1. Emilie 191
I.2.3. Sloane 203
I.2.4. Mordred 211

PART III 217

16. New World Disorder 219
17. The Shape of Family 231
18. A Child's Faith 247
19. Geometry Sucks 255
20. Shades of Mordred 267
21. The Shape of War 275
22. Druid Detective Agency 285

Book 2 Preview: 1. Messin' With Sasquatch	295
Also By Theophilus Monroe	303
About the Author	309

Part I

1. Shadows at the Shire

The shadow creature erupted from the forest, a writhing mass of darkness trailing wisps of smoke like a living nightmare. Its red eyes pierced through the gloom, locking onto Merlin with a predatory focus that turned my blood to ice.

This thing wanted my son.

I thrust out my staff, emerald light flaring to life as I planted myself between Merlin and the monster. Emilie yanked Merlin behind her, shielding him with her body while her fingers drifted toward the knife on her hip.

The creature stalked closer, bones jutting from its amorphous body like jagged shards. It moved with an unnatural gait, flickering between shadow and solidity. A low rumble emanated from its maw, a purr of anticipation.

My fingers clenched around my staff. "Shouldn't you be haunting closets or something?"

The creature pounced with a shriek, claws swiping for my face. I ducked and spun my staff, a gust of wind slamming into the creature's side. It absorbed the blow like smoke, then lashed out again.

I barely dodged the next strike. "Who sent you?" I demanded. "Was it Morgana?"

The creature ignored me, fixated on Merlin cowering behind Emilie. She drew her dagger, the blade glinting in the low light.

"Over my dead body," she growled.

The creature screeched, an ear-piercing wail that sent pain ricocheting through my skull. In that split second it darted past me, shadowy claws outstretched toward my son.

Rage boiled through me, hot and visceral.

This thing wanted to hurt my family? Like hell.

With a guttural yell, I summoned a vortex of wind and light. It slammed into the creature's side, sending it careening into a tree with a resounding crack.

"We've got to get Merlin out of here!" Emilie yelled over the howling gale.

I nodded, never taking my eyes off the creature as it peeled itself off the splintered tree trunk. Dark ichor dripped from its fractured limbs, but it showed no sign of pain or fatigue. If anything, my attack had only angered it more.

Its head swiveled unnaturally to fixate on me, eyes burning with hellish light. A rasping snarl emanated from deep within its chest.

I tightened my grip on my staff. No more holding back—it was time to end this.

The surrounding air crackled with power as I summoned the full force of the elements. "Em, take Merlin and go!"

Emilie scooped Merlin into her arms, holding him close as she backed away. His small body trembled against her, his face buried in the crook of her neck.

"It's okay, sweetheart, I've got you," she murmured.

The creature lunged with a guttural shriek, shadowy claws slicing through the space where they had just stood. I thrust my staff forward, a bolt of lightning arcing from the tip to strike the creature directly in its twisted chest. It let out an unearthly wail, convulsing as electricity coursed through its dark form.

I pressed my attack, battering it with gale force winds and blasts of fire. The creature writhed under the onslaught, screeching its fury. But I could see its form growing fainter, dissolving at the edges as my magic took its toll.

With a final, desperate cry, the creature launched itself at me, claws outstretched in a last ditch effort to fulfill its task. I held my ground, calling on the roots beneath the soil to erupt. They burst forth, thick woody tendrils that wrapped around the creature, dragging it down even as it thrashed and struggled.

"This ends now," I growled through gritted teeth. The air crackled as I summoned every last bit of magic left in me, focusing it into one final strike. The elements alone weren't enough. This thing looked like death in the flesh. The answer to something like that?

Pure Awen, the magic of the Tree of Life, the power of creation. The green energy coursed from my staff as I drew it from the moisture in the ground. I couldn't draw on Awen in such an unrefined form anywhere else—but the otherworld nourished these lands. An explosion of emerald energy engulfed the creature, burning away the last of its shadowy essence until nothing remained but silence.

Panting, I turned to see Emilie regarding me with relief and pride, our son held safely in her arms. We had protected him, for now. But as I met my wife's gaze, I knew our trials were far from over. Merlin's destiny still loomed, its call as inexorable as the tide.

This wasn't the first time *someone* had come through the gateways, passing through the fabric of time to end my son's legacy before it began. But there was something different, more unusual about this encounter.

I'd never seen anything like it.

Was it a spirit, or a flesh-and-blood-monster? A bit of both, it seemed. And why had it ventured so close to the shire? The magic here, the wellsprings of Annwn flowing through the land, usually prevented creatures like *this* from encroaching on our little Eden in the Ozarks.

Breathing heavily, I leaned against my staff for support as the adrenaline faded. The woods were still once more, with no sign remaining of the creature that had attacked us. Emilie stepped forward, one arm wrapped protectively around Merlin while the other reached out to me.

"Are you alright?" she asked, concern in her eyes as she looked me over for any injuries.

I managed a weary nod. "Nothing a hot meal and some rest won't fix," I said with a tired smile.

She knew it was a lie. She could see it on my face, and I saw the same worry reflected back at me in hers. But we couldn't show our fear. We couldn't let Merlin know we were afraid.

Because when things like this started happening, especially when it involved our legendary heritage, it didn't end. What we'd encountered in the woods was just the tip of the iceberg.

Someone was behind it. And whoever—or whatever it was—wouldn't be dissuaded so easily.

Swallowing her trepidation, Emilie turned her focus to Merlin. "And how's my little magician? You were so brave back there."

Merlin peered up at us with wide eyes that had seen too much for one so young. He was only ten-years-old, after all. But he gave us a small smile.

My heart swelled, even as it ached at the burden placed on one who should be carefree. I ruffled his hair. "Let's get you home."

The walk back was a quiet one as we each processed the attack in our own way. But as the living oak walls of our shire came into view, the tension in my shoulders eased. Passed down to me from my parents—also druids—this dwelling served as more than just a home. Its roots ran deep into the Otherworld, drawing on ancient magic. The wellspring under our house flowed with the waters of Annwn.

Here, we were supposed to be safe. This was the closest anything threatening had ventured so close to our home in more than a decade.

Merlin immediately ran off to the corner where his supplies waited: a collection of charcoal pencils and one of a dozen "Big Chief" writing tablets.

Most boys Merlin's age were into video games. Sometimes action figures. Merlin wasn't like most boys. More introverted than the person I'd expected he'd become—given his future self's reputation through history. But he had a long way to go.

Whenever he was upset, he drew. Merlin didn't know the full scope of who he'd one day become. Emilie and I thought it best to shield him from that. A boy shouldn't have to grow up with that kind of burden. How do you tell a kid that eventually he'll grow up, become one of the most powerful wizards in history, and will have to leave our world, go back in time, and help raise a young king and his round table knights?

If destiny was really immutable, he'd come to it in time. We'd tell him when the time was right.

Of course, we only *knew* who he truly was because his older seventy-something self had told us before he was born. Emilie and I weren't together. We were just friends. Merlin's biological mother, Joni, had burdens of her own. A heritage that bound her to a kingdom of merfolk in the Caribbean. It was a call she couldn't decline. And it was the unique combination of Joni's heritage, and mine, that gave Merlin such power. A power he'd grow into in time.

My "sacred" duty was to protect the young boy until he came of age. That's what he told me, anyway. But I knew it was more than that. I was a father. That came first. Sacred duties and destines would take care of themselves.

I'd loved Emilie since we were children. She liked me too, I suppose. It was one of those situations where we both wanted to be together but were too damn afraid of messing up our friendship that neither of us made a move.

But when Joni left, and I had our son, Emilie came to our rescue. She was more than my wife. She'd become a bard. With her songs and instruments, she could cast visions of the tales of old. She could get glimpses of the future. Sometimes, in a fight, if she had her violin, her magic gave me a split-second precognitive advantage. I'd see an enemy's attack *just* before it happened.

But it had been a few years since we'd had to fight much of anything. We were druids. Fighting wasn't in our nature. We loved peace. We revered the wild. We honored balance.

But if we had to fight, we could unleash the earth's fury, and the powers of the otherworld, to protect what was good.

Emilie wrapped an arm around my waist.

I took a deep breath, centering myself in the warmth and light that filled our home. But the peace was short-lived.

"Dad! Mom!" Merlin came barreling back into the room, his over-sized drawing tablet clutched in his hands. "That monster. I've seen it before. In my drawings."

He thrust the tablet at us eagerly. Emilie and I exchanged a glance as we took in the contents that had our son so enthralled.

Charcoal covered page after page, each one filled with meticulous sketches of the shadow creature we had just faced. Every twisted limb, every jagged edge, was captured in perfect detail by Merlin's small hand.

I sucked in a sharp breath. It was one thing for a child to scribble imagined monsters, but the precision of these drawings sent a chill down my spine. Merlin had never seen the creature before today, yet he had replicated it flawlessly... as if he had studied it closely.

"How...how did you draw this?" Emilie asked gently.

Merlin shrugged, his brow furrowing. "I just saw it in my head and had to put it on paper. I thought it was cool, but..."

Cool was not the word I would use. Foreboding settled in my gut as the pieces clicked into place. This was no coincidence. The attack, the drawings... something bigger was at play here. Emilie met my gaze, the same realization dawning in her eyes.

Our son was special. Gifted. And there were dark forces in this world that would seek to snuff out his light before it ever had a chance to shine. But we wouldn't let them. And not just because destiny had plans for Merlin... because he was *our son*.

I ruffled Merlin's hair, giving him my best attempt at a reassuring smile despite the dread coiling within me. "It's an incredible drawing, kiddo. But I think it's time for bed now."

Merlin's face fell. "But I'm not tired!"

Emilie wrapped an arm around his shoulders. "I know, sweetheart. But it's been a long day. Let's get you tucked in."

As she led Merlin upstairs, I began securing protective wards around the shire. I traced runes of shielding into the oak walls, whispering words of fortification. A soft glow emanated from the markings, activating the magic.

It wouldn't be enough. I could feel it in my bones. Something dark was coming for my son, and mere walls would not keep it at bay.

Emilie returned downstairs, her expression grim. We both knew sleep would not come easily tonight.

"The signs are clear," I said. "Merlin's destiny is emerging. And there are those who wish to stop it."

Emilie nodded. "If only we knew who... or what."

I clenched my fists. As a druid, I was sworn to walk in balance with all life. But if someone threatened my family again, they would see nothing but fury.

"We'll find out," I vowed. "And we'll be ready."

No matter what came for him, I'd keep him safe. Merlin would fulfill his destiny. I would make sure of it.

Even if I had to tear the world apart.

2. Charcoal Prophecies

Pink magic swirled around the room like cotton candy, whipping from Emilie's violin. I watched as she dragged the bow across the strings, her eyes closed in concentration as the haunting melody filled the air.

Part of me wanted to snatch the instrument from her hands. I knew where this song would lead, the visions it would summon in our son's fragile mind. But he was seeing things already. He'd drawn the shadow monster before it appeared. If we didn't learn something, there was no telling what was coming next.

We needed answers, and Emilie's bardic power represented our best chance of getting them.

Merlin sat cross-legged on the floor, his tablet and charcoals laid out before him. His wide blue eyes followed the rosy wisps as they curled around him. I could see the fear and uncertainty in those eyes. He knew what was coming too.

"It's okay," I said, laying a hand on his shoulder. "Your mother and I are right here. We won't let anything happen."

He nodded, a brave smile on his lips even as his hands trembled. Emilie's song grew louder, and the magic tightened its grasp on the boy. He picked up a charcoal stick and drew.

I held my breath, praying to any god that would listen that we weren't making a mistake. That the visions summoned would provide the answers we sought and not leave deeper scars on my son's psyche.

Only time would tell, it seemed. For now, all I could do was watch, wait, and hope. Because if we *didn't* get answers, and someone really was after my son, the consequences would be far graver.

Merlin's hand moved furiously across the page, bringing the images in his mind to life. I watched with bated breath as the sketch took form—the shadowy creature from his previous drawings, but now with more detail. Disturbing, spindly limbs ending in jagged claws. Empty, glowing eyes. An aura of malice radiating from the parchment.

My eyes darted over the background details Merlin added. A copse of trees. The edge of a pond. A walking path. With a start, I recognized the location-Forest Park. A creature like the one that attacked us emerged from a small hill at the base of a towering oak.

Not just any oak. The oak I had planted there myself, long ago. An acorn from the Tree of Life, meant to form a gateway between worlds. But now, something far more sinister had come through.

I met Emilie's worried gaze. If evil had corrupted the gateway, it meant something dark was stirring.

And Merlin was caught at the center of it all.

We had to get to the bottom of this. Had to find who or what was behind these creatures being unleashed. And we had to do it fast, before anyone else got hurt. Before they came for Merlin again.

My hands curled into fists as determination flooded through me. We would find answers. We would keep our son safe. No matter what we had to do.

Emilie's voice broke the tense silence. "If that's the tree you think it is, then the gate under it must have changed. The address... or whatever... must have changed. It's not connected to Annwn anymore."

I nodded grimly. She was right. No benevolent creature could come through a gateway to the Otherworld. Something had corrupted it.

Emilie set her violin down, but Merlin kept sketching feverishly. He flipped through his tablet, finding other renderings of the shadow monster, adding details he hadn't imagined before. His small hand flew over the parchment, charcoal staining his fingers.

Then I saw it.

Bodies. Broken, bloodied corpses littering the scenes.

Bile rose in my throat. What horrors was he witnessing in his mind's eye? My instinct as a father was to tear the parchment away, to shelter him if I could. But I couldn't rip the visions from his mind. I was powerless to stop it.

I watched from over his shoulder as my boy continued to add grim details to his sketches. Emilie hovered at my side, tension radiating from her slight frame.

The creatures Merlin drew were not all the same. Their forms shifted subtly in each scene—wispy, smoky, undulating shadows. But the malice was a constant. Oozing menace dripped from Merlin's frantic sketches.

One showed the thing emerging from a sewer grate downtown. Another had it slithering out from an abandoned warehouse. The corpses were different too—an old homeless man splayed on some steps, a jogger crumpled in an alley.

"Are these visions of the future?" Emilie whispered. "Or have these attacks already happened?"

I scanned the images. The locations were too ordinary to place. But the bodies... a chill crept down my spine. They had a horrible realness to them.

"I don't know..." Dread gnawed at my gut. "But I think we need to find out."

I squeezed Emilie's hand, then pulled out my phone. Time to scan the local reports. Bodies don't turn up in a condition like that in a public space and get ignored. I wanted to see if Merlin's drawings matched any recent reports.

Emilie hovered anxiously as I scrolled through the local news sites and police reports. It didn't take long to find what I dreaded—a string of unexplained deaths over the past week.

The first was a homeless man, throat torn out, found near the bus terminal downtown. Just like Merlin's drawing with the sewer grate. Next, a jogger in Riverside Park, mauled beyond recognition. Her mangled body matched the crumpled figure in the alley sketch perfectly.

One after another, each attack corresponded to a scene from Merlin's visions. I pointed them out to Emilie, whose eyes widened in dismay.

"Why?" she whispered. "What's the rhyme or reason? Why kill people at random and *then* come after Merlin? We're a couple of hours away from any of these killings."

I shook my head grimly. "This is no coincidence. The victims were chosen for a reason. Someone... or some*thing*... is behind this."

Emilie shivered, arms wrapped around herself. Then her gaze hardened with determination. "We have to find who. And we have to stop them."

I nodded. The attacks circled the park, centered on the oak.

The attack outside our home was the outlier. And if I hadn't been there...

Our only lead was the tree at Forest Park. Somehow, these creatures had emerged from the portal there. If we were going to discover the truth, that's where we had to begin.

I grabbed my coat and turned to Emilie. "Let's go. We're heading to the park."

Emilie quickly gathered her things, her brow furrowed in thought. "If the attacks all surround your tree, do you think the gateway has been corrupted somehow? Could something from... elsewhere... be coming through?"

I ushered her out to the truck, my mind racing. "It's possible. The alignments between worlds shift. Nothing I know of in Annwn could do this."

Emilie shivered again as she climbed into the passenger seat. Her fingers worried at a loose thread on her shirt, betraying her nerves.

I pressed harder on the gas pedal, gravel spraying from my tires as I weaved through the remote roads surrounding the shire. We'd get answers, one way or another. The sacred oak guarded its secrets, but it would surrender them to me.

3. Poop Emoji

THE HIGHWAY STRETCHED BEFORE us like a river of asphalt, the dotted lines an endless current pulling us forward. Merlin's voice drifted up from the backseat, his curiosity unfettered by the gravity of our quest.

"Are we there yet?"

I chuckled despite myself. "Not yet, buddy. Still more than an hour to go."

My fingers closed around the sigil stone in the cupholder, tracing the three rays embossed into the amber surface. It was smooth and cool, yet seemed to thrum with an energy all its own—my last lingering connection to Dad. My parents died before I'd even reached puberty. It felt like yesterday. I didn't believe it when they told me. Even now, there were times when I half expected them to come waltzing through the door. The stone contained my father's memories, an emanation of who he used to be. It wasn't really him, not his true spirit—but all his knowledge and wisdom was there. All I had to do to access it was channel a little magic into the stone. I'd black out if I did it. I couldn't do it while I was driving. But just *having* it there, touching the amber sigil, dulled my anxiety.

"You okay?" Emilie asked, nodding to the stone. Her violin lay across her lap, polished wood glowing in the sunlight.

"Just thinking about Dad," I said.

Emilie gave my hand a gentle squeeze. "We'll figure this out, like we always do."

"I don't know. People are dying, Em. Dying because of some shadow monster we know nothing about." I kept my voice low so Merlin wouldn't overhear. "And we're the only ones equipped to handle this. The cops won't have a clue about what they're really dealing with. It's our responsibility."

I nodded, keeping my eyes on the road. Emilie was right - we'd get through this together, like we always did. Still, the weight of responsibility sat heavy on my shoulders.

From the backseat, Merlin piped up. "I spy with my little eye something green!"

Despite the circumstances, I couldn't help but smile. Leave it to Merlin to lighten the mood.

Emilie grinned, joining in on the game. "Is it a tree?"

"Nope!" Merlin said.

"How about that sign back there?" I asked.

"No, you'll never guess it," Merlin said slyly.

"Oh yeah? I bet it's the grass," I said.

Merlin laughed. "Be more specific! Which blade?"

I shook my head, chuckling. "Buddy, we're driving. There's no way I can see a single blade."

"It was one we passed a while ago," Merlin said. "So I win!"

Emilie and I shared an amused look. Leave it to a ten-year-old to rig the rules of his own game to make it impossible to lose. The levity was welcome. Just like that, the darkness lifted, if only for a moment.

FINALLY, THE GATEWAY ARCH and the towering skyscrapers of St. Louis' skyline came into view, signaling our arrival. The city buzzed with life as cars honked and people bustled along the sidewalks. We weaved through the labyrinth of streets until we reached Forest Park, a sprawling oasis on the west side of the city.

I parked the truck in a shaded spot near a row of towering oak trees. The three of us stepped out, stretching our legs after the long drive. The air was thick with humidity and the scent of freshly cut grass mingled with the distant smell of fried food from a nearby fair. Children's laughter filled the air as they played on swings and slides at a playground on the periphery of the park. It all seemed so normal, so mundane.

But there was something in the air. Something I didn't like. It wasn't quite palpable—but it was there. As we made our way across the running trails toward the oak I'd planted a decade before, a nausea settled into my gut. Merlin reached for my hand.

"Is something wrong, Dad?" Merlin asked, concern etched on his boyish face. "You look like you're gonna puke."

I gave him a reassuring smile, trying to mask the unease that had settled within me. "Just a little queasy from the long drive, buddy. Don't worry about it."

Even as I said it, though, it felt like a lie. I wasn't usually prone to carsickness. The discomfort was so subtle, though, that I didn't want to jump to conclusions. But my instinct told me the tree and the dark magic behind the shadow monster had something to do with it.

Merlin's grip tightened around my hand, as if he could sense the underlying tension. "I don't feel so good either," he admitted, his voice barely a whisper. "My head. It hurts a little."

Emilie's brow furrowed with worry as she glanced between us. "I feel fine. I'm usually the one susceptible to motion sickness. If this has something to do with the tree…"

Nodding, I made a quick decision. "Em, stay back with Merlin. I'll check out the tree myself. It might be dangerous."

I could see in Emilie's face that she wanted to protest, but her sigh revealed she knew it was the right thing to do. It was one thing for me to risk myself—but we couldn't put our son in danger. If this strange sickness had anything to do with the tree, the closer we got, the worse it would affect us.

"Remember our emojis," Emilie said. We'd had a system, like a little person code, to send each other whenever we were separated. We'd developed the system years ago. Just in case we were in a pinch and needed to let the other person know but weren't in a position to type out a detailed message. While it had been a long time since we'd dealt with any direct threats, when you know about all the supernatural nasties out there that could do you harm, it's good to have a system in place. "The poop emoji if shit's hitting the fan, but not yet an emergency. It means you're in a squeeze, but to stay put for now. The skull emoji if it's a life and death situation. Send that one and I'll be back in a second."

Emilie nodded. "And a heart if all is well and back to normal."

"And the eggplant if I'm feeling frisky. I remember."

Emilie smirked. "Just make sure you have vibrate turned on in case you don't hear the alert."

I knew all the protocol. But it didn't hurt to remind me five or twenty times about anything important. If Emilie ever told me she needed something, I had a tendency to only remember the last couple of things she mentioned. It was pretty bad when I was going to the store. If she didn't remind me, or send me with a list, I'd inevitably forget something.

When we were back at the shire, it was a big deal. Because the closest grocery store was an hour away.

Forgetting to have my notifications turned on my phone to receive her alert would be a classic Elijah mistake. So, I double checked my phone settings, and sure enough, vibrate was off. "Fixed."

"Good thing you checked." Emilie winked at me.

I nodded and returned my phone to my front pocket. "If you feel so much as the slightest threat out here..."

"Poop emoji it is. The skull if the threat is imminent."

I kissed Emilie on the forehead and squeezed Merlin's hand before setting off toward the oak tree alone.

Taking a deep breath, I continued down the trail. We were still maybe a quarter mile away from the tree, but every step was heavier than the last. I retrieved my phone and sent Emilie three eggplants. Just for fun.

She replied with an eye-roll emoji.

I continued down the path. With each stride, the twisting in my stomach intensified, and my head throbbed with a dull ache. It was like walking into a wall of resistance, an invisible force that pushed against me, like trying to walk upstream against a river's current.

As I continued on, several runners jogged past me, effortlessly moving with no resistance at all. It was as if someone specifically wanted to keep *me* away from the gateway at the tree.

I gritted my teeth, fighting against the invisible barrier that seemed to grow stronger with each passing moment. Sweat dripped from my brow, mingling with the humidity in the air. People passed me by, their gazes shifting from curiosity to concern as they witnessed my struggle. They probably thought I was a real jackass, or on drugs. But it didn't matter what they thought. Why worry about strangers' opinions, anyway?

But then, as if in response to my defiance, the resistance vanished. It dissipated so quickly that I stumbled forward, almost falling on my face. A sense of relief flooded through me as I pressed on toward the tree. The throbbing in my head subsided, and the nausea in my gut gradually dissipated.

What the hell?

A sharp scream interrupted my momentary confusion.

My head snapped towards the general direction of the scream, and without a second thought, I took off running towards the sound. The urgency in that cry was undeniable, and my instincts kicked into overdrive.

As I sprinted through the dense foliage of the forest, leaves rustling beneath my feet, my mind raced with possibilities. Who could be in trouble? The timing of the magic resistance I felt dissipating and the scream couldn't be a coincidence. This wasn't a mugging. It couldn't be a common accident. My mind went back to Merlin's sketches, the grim murders he'd depicted in charcoal. If I encountered another shadow monster, I knew how to take it down. I did it once before.

The only thing I knew for sure was that *someone* needed help. I fired off a quick "poop" emoji to Emilie. Just to let her know *something* was going down, but to remind her to stay squatting where she was.

The adrenaline flowed through my veins, fueling my steps as I pushed myself to go faster. Branches whipped against my arms, leaving angry red scratches in their wake. But I barely felt the pain. All that mattered was reaching whoever was in distress.

It was as if the woods were closing in around me. Not because of anything magical. I just wasn't accustomed to running so hard, so fast.

A cramp had already set in under my ribs by the time I arrived on the scene.

I skidded to a halt, my eyes widening at the sight before me. In the middle of a small clearing, amidst the tall grass and wildflowers, sat a woman huddled on the ground. Tremors rocked her body, causing her to shake uncontrollably. Her face was buried in her arms, the rise and fall of her shoulders indicating the depth of her sobs.

Sirens wailed in the distance, their echoing cries mingling with the sounds of nature. It was clear that she had called for help—the phone beside her on the grass was open, connected to a 911 operator. The voice on the other end pleaded for her confirmation that she was still on the line, but she seemed oblivious to their words.

Cautiously, I approached her, my heart pounding in my chest. "Hey," I called out gently, my voice barely above a whisper. "Are you okay?"

The woman looked up, her tear-streaked face revealing a mix of fear and desperation. She gasped for air, struggling to compose herself. "I'm here," she said, her voice shaking. But I couldn't be sure if she was responding to me or the 911 operator.

My eyes scanned the clearing, searching for the source of her terror. And then I saw it—an image that sent a chill down my spine. A mangled body hung from a gnarled tree branch, suspended by a black vine. Limbs torn from the torso lay scattered around the base of the tree. It was a gruesome sight, the stuff of nightmares.

I knelt down beside the woman, careful not to startle her further. "What happened?" I asked softly, my heart heavy with sorrow for both the victim and this woman who had witnessed such horror.

She took a deep breath, her voice trembling as she forced out a few words. "You wouldn't believe me. I don't know what I saw."

"Do you know that person? The one who was attacked?"

The woman shook her head, tears streaming down her face. "No, I've never seen them before. I was just out for a walk... then I saw this... it happened so fast."

She trailed off, unable to find the words to describe her terror.

"What's your name?" I asked, hoping to establish some semblance of a connection. Forcing a small smile, I added, "I'm Elijah. I heard your screams and came to help."

"Hello, ma'am?" The voice came from her phone. It was the 911 operator. "Are you alright, ma'am?"

"Yes, sorry. I'm still here."

"Do you feel safe? Someone is with you?"

"A stranger. He seems nice. I think…"

"We should probably get you somewhere safe," I added. "We need to get closer to the trail, around more people."

"That's what I'd advise as well," the operator added. "I'll be here until the police get there. They should be just a few minutes out."

I pressed my lips together. I couldn't exactly ask this woman—whoever she was—to hang up on 911. But whatever she saw, she wasn't likely to tell me, if she ever would, if the operator was listening in.

When people see something supernatural, they tend toward denial. It's a lot easier—as disconcerting as it sounds—for most people to think they're losing their mind than come to grips with the truth of the supernatural world. Especially when they see something so terrifying. And if one of those shadow monsters was involved, it was unlikely she'd tell anyone. Unless someone could give her reason to believe she *wasn't* crazy.

I hesitated a moment. Confirming the truth to this woman would have long-lasting effects. But I knew if I didn't get an answer, somehow, I'd never convince her to talk later. Even if I figured out how to get in touch with the woman after the cops finished at the scene.

I still had one of Merlin's drawings in my jacket pocket. I pulled it out and gestured toward it. I didn't want to say anything out loud. I wasn't sure what the 911 operator would think if we started talking about monsters. Anything we said would be recorded and likely examined by the police later.

I was also keenly aware of the fact that as the only other person on the scene if I said anything at all fishy I could quickly move from "witness" status to "suspect."

The woman's eyes widened. She gasped. Her hand instinctively went to her mouth. She looked at me with tear-filled eyes and nodded. That told me all I needed to know. She'd seen what I thought she saw.

But now we had no choice. She'd witnessed something horrible. The police were going to want to know what she saw; they'd want me to tell them how I came upon this woman after what happened and if I'd seen anything. Neither of us could tell the cops we'd seen a monster.

So I pulled out my phone and started to type out a message. I finished and showed her the screen.

All you saw was a shadow. It's not a lie. This isn't the first attack by something like this and I'm here to help. But the police will never believe you if you tell them the complete truth.

The woman wiped a tear from her eyes. "The name's Karen. Thank you, Elijah. I wish I knew what happened. But all I saw... was a shadow... and by the time I realized what happened, it was gone."

It was out there. Now she just had to stick to the story. The cops wouldn't be able to solve the case. They'd certainly try. But at least I'd learned a few things. The shadow monster we'd seen at the shire *was* connected to the tree in the park. The sickening energy Merlin and I both sensed when we arrived had something to do with the creature's malevolence. Once the attack ended, the energy faded.

I still needed to examine the tree. But I couldn't leave Karen alone. I deleted the message I'd typed out for her benefit and send a text to Emilie instead. This was going to take a while. But I'd meet back up with them as soon as I could.

4. Don't be a Karen

Karen paced the leaf-strewn sidewalk, phone clutched in her shaking hand. "They said three minutes five minutes ago!"

I scanned the surrounding woods, every sense on high alert. Something sinister lurked within the looming pines, the birdsong muted.

The pounding between my temples returned with a vengeance. I winced, pressing my fingers to my head. The nausea roiled in my gut. Not again.

The static-filled voice of the 911 operator crackled from the phone's speaker. "Units en route. Please stay on the line."

Karen exhaled in relief. But she wasn't feeling what I was. The cops wouldn't know how to handle a goddamn shadow monster. I couldn't exactly throw down druid style against one in front of the authorities.

But I couldn't leave Karen defenseless either.

A flicker of darkness flashed in my peripheral vision. I wasn't sure if it was another shadow monster or my pain-stricken head playing tricks on me. Karen paled, following my gaze. The look on her face confirmed my worst suspicion. She must have glimpsed it, too.

My phone buzzed in my pocket. I fished it out, heart sinking as I read Emilie's text.

Merlin's headache is worsening fast. He needs you NOW.

"Shit," I muttered under my breath. If that thing was after my boy next...

I met Karen's terrified eyes. "Listen, I need to go check on my son. He's in danger." Her mouth fell open in protest, but I raised a hand. "The police are almost here. You'll be safe." I gentled my voice, unsure if I even believed my own words while I held her shoulders. "All you saw was a shadow, okay? Nothing more. If something is out there, I'll stop it before it gets to you, okay?"

She nodded jerkily, eyes brimming with tears.

I took off at a dead sprint, pulse thundering in my ears.

I raced through the woods, following the tug in my gut towards Merlin. My head pounded with each hurried step, but I pushed through the pain. I had to get to my son.

I stumbled into the small clearing where I'd left him and Emilie. Merlin was curled up on the park bench, head in Emilie's lap. She looked up, relief flooding her face when she saw me.

"Dad!" Merlin cried. "My head really hurts."

I kneeled in front of him, brushing his curls back to feel his forehead. He was clammy but didn't seem to have a fever.

"I know, kiddo. We're going to figure this out." I looked over his head and met Emilie's worried gaze. She didn't have to say it. We both knew this wasn't just a normal headache.

I stood, ruffling Merlin's hair before stepping away. Emilie followed me out of earshot.

"I feel it, too. But it's not as bad here as it is further into the park. It might be coming from my tree," I said in a low voice. "But maybe not. If I follow the pain..."

Emilie's eyes widened. She glanced back at our son, who had curled into a tiny ball on the bench.

"Be careful," she whispered, gripping my arm.

I pulled her in for a quick, fierce hug. "I'll stop this thing before it hurts anyone else. Stay with Merlin."

I raced through the trees, following the increasing nausea and pounding headache like a twisted compass. With every step, the sensations grew worse, confirming my suspicions that whatever dark magic was summoning these shadow beasts lay ahead.

I knew where the pain was leading me. I wasn't far from that tree...

I burst into the clearing, skidding to a halt at the sight before me. The great oak, once a proud sapling grown from the acorn of the Tree of Life, was now corrupted. Its leaves were shriveled and black, its trunk oozing a foul ichor. Dark magic swirled around it in malignant currents.

And surrounding the stricken tree was a circle of figures in crimson robes, their faces obscured by hoods. They held hands, chanting in a language that grated painfully against my ears. The tree's writhing magic flowed into them as they chanted, feeding on its power.

A rage boiled up in me. The heat that spread through my brow did little to help with the pain. This was my tree. The offspring of the Tree of Life. It was sacred. It guarded what used to be a connection between this world and Annwn—what some know as the Garden of Eden itself.

Moving quickly, I pulled my staff from my pocket. Channeling my druidic magic, it expanded to full size in my hand. I swept it around me in an arc, calling on the spirits of the forest.

The corrupted tree fought against me, but the surrounding woods responded. I heard the trees' voices crying out in a language without words. A shared agony from the evil permeating this place. But beneath the pain, they expressed their willingness to aid me however they could.

Gripping my staff, I prepared to unleash the magic of nature against these violators. But I had to be swift—lives depended on it.

"Stand down!" I shouted, as green energy swirled and crackled around me.

The chanting figures turned, breaking their circle. I glimpsed a strange geometric symbol embroidered on their robes in gold thread. Like a dozen or more overlapping circles all encompassed in a larger circle. From a distance, it almost resembled a honeycomb, but not quite. Maybe a flower.

Their leader stared at me, his face lost in the shadows of his hood. "Do not interfere, Druid," he intoned. "This is none of your concern."

"You attacked my son!" I shot back. "You're hurting innocent people. Like hell this isn't my concern."

I swept my staff toward them, calling on the vines and branches around us. They strained toward the cultists, seeking to bind them, to stop them.

But some dark force around the robed figures repelled my efforts. The forest couldn't penetrate their dark barrier.

I narrowed my eyes. I would not be deterred so easily. These desecrators had chosen the wrong wood for their foul ritual.

"You have no idea who you're dealing with," I told them, readying another strike. I would keep trying for as long as it took. I had to stop them, no matter the cost.

Then a bloodcurdling scream pierced the air, followed by the crack of gunshots.

My head jerked up. The sounds had come from the direction of the road, where I'd left Karen waiting for the police.

The cult leader seized on my distraction. "What will it be, druid?" he asked, a sly note in his voice. "Will you continue to flail against us pointlessly? Or will you help those poor people?"

He swept a hand toward the continuing screams. "I'd hate for you to have their blood on your hands."

I clenched my jaw, torn. I couldn't let these bastards succeed with their vile ritual. What the hell were they trying to accomplish? It wasn't good. I knew that much. But I couldn't ignore those screams. People were in danger.

"I don't know who the hell you are," I bit out. "Or what you hope to gain here. But this isn't over."

The cultists laughed, a chorus of scorn. "Oh, I suspect it's not," their leader replied.

Cursing under my breath, I turned and sprinted toward the sounds of struggle. I had to hope I could stop the creature and protect the police long enough to return and finish things here.

My mind raced as I ran, seeking solutions. But one thought rose over all others: I could not let these dark sorcerers succeed. The appearance of those murderous shadow monsters and the cultists' ritual around the tree didn't coincide by happenstance. No matter what it took, I had to stop them before they completed their goal, before they hurt anyone else.

5. Reasonable Doubt

Leaving the cultists to their dark ritual, I took off running towards the screams and gunshots echoing through the park. With each pounding step, pain throbbed in my temples from the dark magic saturating the area. I pushed through it, focused on finding the source of the commotion.

A bullet suddenly whizzed past my face, missing me by inches and embedding itself into a nearby tree with a loud crack. I whipped around to see a shadowy figure dart across the path, moving faster than my eyes could track. The gunshot must have come from someone else. I scanned the area, but couldn't spot the shooter.

Gritting my teeth against the blinding headache, I pursued the shadow monster. It slipped between trees and underbrush with preternatural speed, but I matched its pace. As it emerged into a moonlit clearing, I halted and, using the glow on my staff like a sparkler, drew a rune in the air. Glowing chains of light materialized and lashed out, ensnaring the thrashing beast. It let out an unearthly wail as the chains burned away its shadowy essence.

These shadow monsters weren't so hard to defeat now that I knew what to do. But the cops wouldn't stand a chance. If I'd learned anything from watching *Indiana Jones* movies growing up—an archaeologist with a gun beats the best-trained swordsman. You don't bring a knife to a gunfight. You can't bring a gun to a magical battle. It won't do much good. If the police pursued these cultists, there'd be a massacre.

I turned to head back towards the ritual site, but before I could take a step, a stern voice called out—

"Freeze! Drop the weapon and put your hands up!"

Shit...

A female police officer stood on the path, gun aimed right at me. I quickly set down my oaken staff and raised my hands.

"It's not a weapon, just a walking stick," I said evenly.

"I don't care what it is, kick it here now!" she barked. I complied and kicked the staff away from me.

"What are you doing out here?" she demanded. Her eyes were sharp, taking in every detail. This was no rookie cop.

"You're here responding to the 911 call," I explained calmly. "I was helping Karen, the woman who called it in. Check with dispatch, they'll confirm."

The officer's gaze remained steely. "Maybe so. But that doesn't explain what you're doing traipsing around in these woods."

I hesitated. How could I explain this in a way she'd believe?

"I heard something in the trees," I said finally. "There's already a body hanging in the trees. I figured if it's the killer, it might be the best chance to catch him."

The cop raised an eyebrow. "You went after a suspected killer empty-handed?"

"You don't understand," I backpedaled. "My son and wife are just on the other side of the park. I was worried that the killer might come upon them. I just figured maybe I could stop him. At the very least, distract him enough to keep people safe until you guys arrived."

The officer cocked an eyebrow. "Your family is out here?"

"I need to find them, make sure they're alright," I pressed urgently. "Please, officer, I have to go."

"I'm afraid I can't let you do that," the officer said firmly. "This is an active crime scene. We need to secure the area. Where is your family?"

I nodded in the direction where they were. "At a park bench off the running path. About a hundred yards that way."

She put a hand on her radio. "Dispatch, we have civilians in the southwest quadrant of the park. Send a unit to escort them out of the park."

She clipped the radio back onto her belt. "My officers will make sure your family gets to safety. But you need to come with me, put your hands above your head."

I sighed in frustration. How could I make her understand?

"Look, I'm not the bad guy here," I said evenly. "You fired your weapon back there. Clearly, you saw something that spooked you. What was it?"

The officer tilted her head, narrowing her eyes. "There was movement in the trees ahead. I had reason to believe someone was approaching in a threatening manner. I did what was necessary."

"So you fired without actually seeing what you were shooting at?" I challenged. "Is that proper protocol?"

The cop's expression hardened. "I don't have to explain myself to you, sir. Now, for the last time, put your hands above your head."

I ran a hand through my hair in exasperation. I didn't have time for this dance. Every minute I wasted was another minute for those cultists to complete their ritual.

I took a deep breath and tried a different tactic.

"Look, I know what you saw back there rattled you," I said gently. "You encountered something you can't rationally explain. I get it. But you have to trust me when I tell you I'm the only one who can stop this. There's evil at work here. And this isn't the first case with death like this. I can help end this."

The officer's eyes widened fractionally. For a moment, I thought I was getting through to her. But then she schooled her features back into a mask of skepticism.

"That's not my concern right now," she said briskly. "My job is to secure the scene and make sure there are no continuing threats. Now, are you going to come along peacefully or not?"

I clenched my jaw in frustration. Time for the direct approach.

"There's a group of people deeper in these woods performing some kind of dark ritual," I said urgently. "They're the ones behind these killings. Let me stop them!"

The officer considered me for a long moment. I held my breath, willing her to believe me. To trust her instincts about what she'd seen.

But then she shook her head. "We'll send officers to investigate your claim. But right now, I need you to put your hands above your head."

Damn. I had no choice left but to play my trump card.

"Regular weapons won't work against these people," I warned. "Trust me, I've dealt with their kind before. Your guns will be useless. I'm the only one who can stop these murders!"

Her eyes narrowed. "Are you threatening to resist arrest, sir?"

"What? No, I just..." I trailed off helplessly. Clearly, reason wasn't getting me anywhere with this cop. I'd have to find another way to get to those cultists.

"Hands above your head," the officer repeated firmly. "Now."

With a resigned sigh, I complied.

The officer stepped behind me and I felt the cold metal of the handcuffs snap around my wrists.

"You're making a mistake," I said, trying one last plea. "Innocent lives are at stake here."

She grabbed my elbow and steered me back down the path. I stumbled a bit, thrown off balance by having my hands bound behind me.

The woods were eerily silent now except for the crunch of leaves under our shoes.

As we emerged from the trees, I spotted the huddled form of Karen speaking with another officer near a squad car. She was wrapped in a shock blanket, mascara streaked down her cheeks from crying. At least she was safe for now.

The officer led me past the crime scene, dotted with fluttering police tape and evidence markers. I kept my eyes forward, not wanting to see what grim scene lay in the clearing. A body bag being loaded into the back of an ambulance was evidence enough.

Karen's head jerked up as I approached. Her eyes went wide with surprise.

"That's him!" she cried, rising unsteadily to her feet. "The man who saved me. Why are you arresting him?"

The officer ignored her outburst, continuing to lead me toward the second waiting squad car.

I glanced back at Karen, silently willing her to trust that I had a plan. But right now, my hands were tied—literally—and I had no way of getting through to the detective. As we approached the waiting squad car, I noticed a flicker of movement near the edge of the woods.

A hooded figure stood partially concealed behind a tree, watching us intently. My heart raced, recognizing the dark aura that emanated from him. This was one of the cultists, likely monitoring the situation to ensure their ritual remained undisturbed.

I almost spat out the cultist's location. He was among those responsible—the *real* killers. But if I pointed the cops in his direction, I only put *them* in danger.

"Look, officer. I'm a witness, not a suspect. Your other witness just confirmed as much!"

The officer retrieved my wallet from my pocket and examined my license. "Mr. Wadsworth. We'll make that determination soon enough. But for now, you need to come with us."

"But my family!" I protested.

"I already sent a unit to ensure their safety. They'll be fine. My officers will let them know you're with us."

I sat in the back of the squad car, handcuffed and frustrated. My mind raced with thoughts of Emilie and Merlin. Were they really safe? The cops wouldn't be able to protect them if another one of those monsters came upon them.

I clenched my fists, feeling the magic humming just beneath my skin. Most of my spells were carved in sigils on the staff. I still had a few abilities I could use if push came to shove. Spells I'd cast enough that I could do them by second-nature without my staff focusing my power. But most of the spells that were worth using in a fight I hadn't needed to use in years. I was out of practice. I *needed* my staff. Without my staff, my magic was... unpredictable and unwieldy.

The squad car jolted as it turned a corner, and I glimpsed the hooded figure disappearing into the shadows of the trees. The cultist had been watching, waiting. The realization hit me like a physical blow. They knew I was in custody. Would they use this opportunity to strike at Merlin?

The police officer who'd arrested me glanced at me in the rearview mirror, her eyes guarded. Her partner—a man in his mid-thirties with a bulging gut—sat beside her. I needed to convince her of the danger lurking in those woods, waiting to unleash chaos upon innocents.

"Officer, please," I began, my voice earnest. "I understand that you have protocols to follow, but I need you to trust me on this. There are lives at stake in those woods, innocent lives. Your officers can't protect my family! I may not have been able to convince you earlier, but I know there is something much darker at play here than meets the eye."

The detective's grip on the steering wheel tightened, her knuckles turning white. She shot me a quick glance, gauging my sincerity.

Her partner turned over his shoulder and looked at me with a cocked eyebrow. "Are you really going to stick to that story?"

I narrowed my eyes. "Doesn't matter. You haven't read me my rights. That means nothing I say before you do is admissible."

The partner looked back at the officer who'd arrested me. "Damn it, Harding. You're a seasoned detective. Don't tell me you *forgot* to read this guy his rights."

The detective shook her head. "I don't think he's a suspect. But I needed him for questioning."

"You found him at the scene of the crime running through the woods. Of course, he's a suspect! You're off your game, Harding. What happened out there?"

The detective cleared her throat. "I'm not sure. But if you want to read him his rights, have at it."

The partner recited my Miranda rights. I had the right to remain silent, right to an attorney, yadda, yadda. I should have kept my mouth shut. Because now, if I said anything at all, they'd be able to use it against me in a court of law.

The thing was, I couldn't afford to remain silent. I had to get back to the woods and stop those cultists. They didn't have any evidence to hold me as a suspect. But if I told them the truth, well, they'd probably lock me up on a psych hold.

All I could do was stick to the barest of facts. "Look, I heard a scream. I thought someone was in trouble. I found Karen, terrified, already on speaker phone with dispatch. I saw the body in the tree. Someone was in the woods and I made a calculated but probably foolish decision to go after whoever it was rather than sit there while a killer stalked us from the cover of the trees."

I'd said more to Detective Harding already. But this was the only thing that was admissible—and it would jibe with anything Karen told them.

If the cultists found my staff out there, I was doubly screwed. They knew I was a druid the moment I confronted them. I didn't know how much they knew about me or how my magic worked, but if they did, well, they'd know that if they took my staff, it would put me at a disadvantage.

But Detective Harding saw something in the park. She shot at that shadow monster before she encountered me. My best chance at getting released in time was to speak to her alone. Without her partner present. Because if she saw what I thought she saw, she'd never admit it in the presence of other cops.

6. A Detective's Dilemma

THE COLD METAL TABLE and hard plastic chair did little to put me at ease as I sat alone in the stark interrogation room. I checked my watch again—nearly an hour had passed since they tossed me in here.

My leg bounced with nervous energy. Were Emilie and Merlin okay? Those cultists were still out there somewhere, and now the cops were involved, too. I took a deep breath in a futile attempt to release the pressure in my chest. It was like they were wrenching a vice on my ribcage. Each minute that passed, they turned it a little tighter. What was going on out there? How were those cloaked men manipulating *my* tree? What was the source of their power? Why were they killing people? And were the cops really blaming me for all of it?

There wasn't a damn thing I could do.

Stuck in this room, I was powerless...

The door finally opened and Detective Harding entered. She was a petite woman with short black hair. She was small, but my brief encounter with her before suggested she wasn't the sort to trifle with. What she lacked in stature, she made up for in demeanor.

Wordlessly, she placed a bottled water on the table in front of me.

I twisted off the cap and took a long swig before fixing her with an intense stare. "My family—are they alright? Have you spoken with them?"

She held my gaze evenly. "Yes, they're here at the station. I just spoke with them."

I scratched the back of my head. "Are you planning to charge me with anything, Detective?"

Detective Harding slid a manila folder across the table to me.

"Take a look at these," she said, her voice flat.

I flipped open the folder. Inside were several large glossy photos, each more gruesome than the last. Mutilated bodies, violent scenes of death. My stomach churned. What kind of head-game was she playing with me?

Stay calm, Elijah. Don't overreact.

"I wasn't in the city when any of these murders happened," I said evenly. "My family and I live deep in the Ozarks. We keep to ourselves."

"How do you know when these killings happened? There's no date on any of the images. And you haven't looked at the rest of the information in the file."

I sighed. "Look, I just got into town today. Whenever these crimes happened, I wasn't around." It wasn't a lie. I had just arrived in town. I also knew it would rouse the detective's suspicions if I said I'd already suspected these killings were connected to the one in the park and that I'd come to town specifically to stop whoever was responsible.

Harding's eyes narrowed, scrutinizing me. "Your wife told me as much. But that proves nothing. A spouse will go to great lengths to cover for her partner."

I shook my head. "Look at my phone. Check my credit card records. You'll find charges and GPS data that will show I haven't been to the city once in the last year. I'm not the guy you're looking for."

The detective's stern exterior cracked a little. She stared at me intently, like she was peering into my soul, extracting information from my psyche I wouldn't willingly yield.

"You took down that thing in the park like it was nothing. Like you'd *done* this before."

I winced. "You saw that, huh?"

"You saved my life, Mr. Wadsworth. You were right before. I shot at that thing because I was scared to death. If you hadn't been there…"

I stood up from the table. "You knew I wasn't the killer, and you arrested me anyway? You hammer me with questions about my whereabouts when you knew all along—"

"It was still suspicious, Mr. Wadsworth. I don't know what you are or how you do the things I saw. But I can't exactly put it in my report that I saw a suspect kill a black monster with a magic stick."

I grinned a little. "Yeah, probably best to keep that to yourself. But I *am* here to help. Tell me you believe that, at least! You said it yourself. I *saved* your life."

The detective pinched her chin. "I need to know how you know about these killers, these monsters, or whatever they are. What brought you to St. Louis? I doubt your arrival at the park was by happenstance."

"One of those monsters attacked my family," I said finally. "I came here to find answers. To find out who's responsible for these killings."

Harding considered this, arms crossed. I couldn't tell if she believed me or not. She'd recently had her entire world rattled by an encounter with something supernatural. Considering that, her composure was impressive. Her expression gave nothing away.

"One of those shadow monsters attacked my *son*, detective. I know you don't understand any of what you saw today. I can't blame you for thinking someone with my... abilities... might be suspect. But if you suspend disbelief for a moment, and you look at my *actions*, there's nothing about what I did in the park that should make me a suspect. Quite the opposite."

"Well, you've certainly got my attention," she said. Her tone made it clear our conversation was far from over.

Harding slid a business card across the table. "Detective Sloane Harding," it read.

I pocketed the card. "I'll keep you updated if I learn more about these killings. But you have to let me walk. I can't stop this thing from a cell."

Harding considered me a moment, then nodded. "Don't make me regret this, Mr. Wadsworth. My superiors catch wind of any of... this..." She waved her hand vaguely. "Let's just say I'm going out on a limb here."

I stood, relief flooding through me. "Thank you, detective. I know how strange this all sounds, but lives are at stake. With your help, I believe I can stop these killings."

Harding led me to the front desk, where an officer handed me my confiscated belongings—including my oaken staff. I sighed in relief. I was afraid the cultists got it.

"I saw what you did to that creature," Harding said quietly as we walked. "I still don't understand how, but that staff... it's important, isn't it?"

"It's a conduit," I explained. "Thank you for retrieving it. It helps me focus my abilities."

Harding shook her head in wonderment. "Abilities... right. I'm trusting you, Mr. Wadsworth. Don't make me regret it."

I met her gaze. "The only thing you'll regret is if you try to stop me from finding these killers. Your superiors don't know what they're up against. I can't say exactly what we're facing, but this kind of thing isn't new to me. I'm the best chance you've got."

Harding crossed her arms. "What are you, exactly, Mr. Wadsworth?"

What am I? I should have expected the question. I wasn't sure how to answer without evoking another twenty questions, so I just laid it out there. "I'm a druid."

"Alright. Whatever that means, you need to be discreet. Stop those responsible, but be careful. If you make one false step... if one more body drops, and there's so much as a thread that connects you to the scene of another incident, I won't be able to protect you."

I nodded. We understood each other. Wordlessly, I turned and pushed through a set of double doors.

I strode into the waiting area, immediately spotting Emilie and Merlin. Emilie leapt up and threw her arms around me, relief etched on her face.

"What happened in there?" she asked anxiously. "Are you in trouble?"

"Not yet," I replied. "That detective, Sloane Harding—she's willing to give me space to operate, for now at least." I turned to Merlin. "How're you feeling, kiddo?"

"I'm okay," he said. "My head doesn't hurt anymore." Then, uncertainly, "Dad, am I in trouble too?"

I knelt down and put my hands on his shoulders. "No, Merlin. You did nothing wrong. But things are dangerous right now, and I need you to listen to me carefully, understand? If you have any visions, any urge to draw anything else, you need to tell me immediately."

He nodded, eyes wide.

"Good." I stood up again. "We need to move fast. The police don't have any real leads yet, but the more bodies that drop, the harder they'll dig. And they won't like what they find." I lowered my voice. "We're dealing with dark forces here. I saw a group of cultists gathered around the tree. Until we know their end-game, we won't have any way to predict who the next victim might be."

Emilie squeezed my hand supportively. "What's our next move?"

I hefted my staff, feeling its power thrum through my fingers. "The detective showed me some files on the other murders. Same MO as the ones I already researched—throats torn out, bodies mangled. No discernible pattern that connects the victims."

Emilie furrowed her brow thoughtfully. "Are we certain these victims were targeted? Could they just have been in the wrong place at the wrong time?"

"I'm not sure either way," I admitted. "But these cultists were willing to summon that horror in a public park. They're ruthless, with no regard for innocent lives." I clenched my fist. "Whether or not it's intentional, they deem these deaths an acceptable cost for whatever sick goal they're pursuing."

Emilie bit her lip. "You have no idea who these cultists are?"

I shook my head. "They recognized me as a druid. So, they know things. They were all dressed in red and had a strange symbol embroidered on their robes."

Emilie glanced at Merlin. "You have your drawing tablet in the truck, right?"

Merlin nodded. "Sure do."

"Can you replicate the symbol?" Emilie asked. "I might be able to use my violin to shed some light on it."

"The symbol was intricate, but I can try. I need to get back to the park. Whatever the cultists are up to, it centers on my tree. There's a lot the surrounding forest might reveal about what's happening, if I ask."

7. Butt Heads in Suits

I slumped back against the worn leather seat of my truck, staring in frustration at the sketchpad in my lap. The symbol those cultists had embroidered on their robes was burned into my mind, but no matter how many times I tried to recreate it on paper, the intricacies eluded me. It was a circle enclosing a bunch of other circles. I wasn't sure how many there were in total or precisely how they intersected. None of my attempts looked quite like what I was visualizing.

"Damn it," I muttered, tossing the pad aside. "The symbols are too complex and I only got a quick look."

Emilie glanced over, her brow furrowing. "Let me see what you've got so far. Maybe I can fill in some blanks with a little bardic intuition."

I flipped back through the pages until I found my best attempt. Though I had little faith it was even close. "Here. But I'm telling you, it's not right. With sigils like this, regardless of whatever kind of warped magic they're using, the devil is in the details. If it's not exact, it won't reveal anything, no matter how hard we try."

She studied the rough sketch, humming tunelessly as she turned it this way and that. "I think I can work with this," she finally pronounced. "We'll just have to hope there are more clues back at the tree in the park. Maybe we can piece together the full symbol."

"Maybe," I agreed half-heartedly, shoving the truck into gear. Emilie handed the sketch pad back to Merlin, who immediately found a blank page and started drawing again. There was no telling any more if what he drew was real, if it had some kind of prophetic quality, or if it was just his youthful imagination at work. He didn't even know. When he drew the shadow monsters before the one attacked us outside our home, he hadn't considered they might be real.

"Any chance you can try to draw around the symbol I made?" I asked. "There's a chance you might intuitively reconstruct it."

Merlin shrugged. "I can try. But I'm really not seeing anything."

"Do your best, honey," Emilie said. "It can't hurt to try."

Emilie was right, of course. She almost always was. I'd never say that out loud. She'd be insufferable if I did.

More than once through the years, she'd given me unsolicited advice that I regrettably ignored to my peril. Long before she was a bard, or I knew I was a druid.

Even when we were children, she had a subtle grasp on what was really going on in a given situation. She saw things I was too dense to recognize.

Not that I was dumb. I just wasn't as *observant* as Emilie. I was introverted by nature. I spent more time in my own head than in the real world.

It wasn't unheard of that someone might have an entire conversation to my face without me comprehending a single word they said. I'd get so *distracted* by my own damn thoughts that I'd forget to listen.

Emilie bought me a t-shirt for last Father's Day that said, "It may look like I'm listening to you, *but in my head*, I'm saving the world."

There was more truth to that than you know.

Emilie *was* right. It didn't hurt to let Merlin try to reconstruct the sigil himself—even though he hadn't seen it in person. We already knew he was connected to all of this *somehow*. We knew his power would one day eclipse mine. Exactly *how* his power would manifest remained a mystery. At least in part.

Until we knew exactly how Merlin's sketch-pad creations interacted with what was going on, there was a chance he'd come up with something crucial we could use.

Whatever that symbol on the cultists' robes meant, finding the answer might be our only way of discovering what was going on and—just as importantly—*who* we were dealing with.

I pulled the truck up to the curb on the far side of the park. The murder earlier happened on the opposite side. Taking Detective Harding's warning seriously, I thought it best to approach the tree from the other direction.

Forest Park is one of the largest urban parks in the United States, spanning 1400 acres. It's home to a museum, the St. Louis Zoo, a golf course, and its fair share of crime. Mostly, though, when dark magic wasn't in the air, it was fairly safe during the day.

We got out and started down a trail through the woods, approaching the ancient gateway tree from the opposite direction.

There was a calm in the air that hadn't been there before. The oppressive illness-inducing energy that had weighed down my senses was gone. In its place was a lightness, a feeling of tranquility emanating from the nature spirits that dwelled here.

Strange. Considering the malevolent energy we'd encountered here earlier, this 180-degree shift was welcome, but unexpected.

Merlin seemed unaffected as well. No headaches or nausea like before. His eyes were bright with curiosity as he took in the woods around us.

"What happened, Dad? It feels so different now," he said.

"I don't know, buddy. But we're gonna find out."

The trees rustled gently in the breeze. Birdsong filled the air. It was as if the events of the morning had never happened at all. It was so pleasant it was *suspicious*. Malevolent magics didn't fade from a place so quickly. They hung around longer than anyone wanted—like that weird uncle at Thanksgiving.

I ruffled my fingers through Merlin's hair and we continued down the forest path, leaves and twigs crunching under our feet. Up ahead, I could see my sacred tree, its branches reaching high into the sunny sky.

As we approached, the transformation amazed me. Where before the tree had appeared sickly, its bark oozing black ichor, now it was the picture of vitality. Its branches were full of verdant green leaves that rustled in the breeze. The trunk was a healthy brown, and I sensed the pure magic of Annwn coursing through it.

I reached out and placed my hand on the bark. Closing my eyes, I focused my druidic senses, trying to detect any remnants of the dark energy from before. But there was nothing. Only the bright song of the lifeforce that flowed from the world beyond the gateway.

How was this possible? In a few hours, it was as if the darkness had been completely cleansed from this place. Had the cultists' spell expired that quickly? Or had something else neutralized their magic in the interim?

I opened my eyes with a furrowed brow. While part of me was relieved the tree and the surrounding forest felt normal again, the rapid shift didn't sit right.

Remember that weird uncle? If he leaves too fast, you can usually be sure he's got *something* planned that isn't altogether wholesome. Because weird uncles—and dark magics—*never* leave before you want them to.

Something bigger was at play here. This return to normalcy was just the calm before the storm.

Emilie must have noticed the concern on my face. She came over and gave my arm a reassuring squeeze.

"What is it?" she asked.

I shook my head. "I'm not sure. But something about this doesn't feel right."

I scanned the surrounding trees, reaching out with my senses. There were no obvious signs of dark magic, but the lingering unease remained.

Emilie followed my gaze. As she surveyed the area, her eyes settled on a large boulder nestled at the base of a towering oak. She tilted her head thoughtfully.

"Do you think that rock might show us what happened here?" she asked.

I raised an eyebrow. Emilie was suggesting we try lithomancy—the divination art of reading stones. It was an obscure practice, even amongst druids, but it ran in my blood. It was how my father had recorded his memory in the sigil stone that still sat in my truck's cupholder.

Certain stones had a way of *recording* events that occurred in their vicinity—especially events that involved the use of magic.

That's one reason many people *think* they see ghosts. A specter might appear doing something routine. Going up and down the stairs, for instance. Sometimes someone will see a spirit that appears to be reliving their death... over and over again.

Talk about a nightmarish way to experience the afterlife.

Except this kind of "residual haunt" isn't really a haunt at all. Most times, it's because of the presence of limestone or other mineral deposits on the property. Running water, like an underground spring, can amplify the phenomenon. It's usually an event in the past that's been *imprinted* or recorded on the stone through either intense or repeated psychological energy.

Everyone has a little magic in them. Most people can't wield it in any fantastic way. But performing a habit or the experience of anguish—like at the moment of someone's death—can leave behind echoes in the stones.

Think of it like this. If you want to carve something into a stone, you can either use a very aggressive instrument to do the job quickly, or you can use something more common to cut away at the stone little by little until a crevice forms. Agony was like an aggressive instrument. Habit was like a dull knife. Both did the job—eventually.

That's how stones worked when they recorded events from the past. Since the cultists had used a dark magic in the area, and since the stone had been accustomed to the magic that emanated from the sacred tree for the last decade-plus, there was probably a lot that the stone could reveal.

"Great idea." I pinched my chin. "Your music, combined with my magic, could coax out the memories stored in the rock."

Emilie nodded, unslinging her violin case from her back. "Then let's give it a shot."

I tightened my grip on my oaken staff as we approached the boulder. This type of divination required intense focus and energy. I would have to channel my druidic power into the stone while Emilie played, opening a window into its buried past.

Though we wouldn't have to go too deep. We were looking for events that occurred just hours before. And if the cultists' activities were responsible for the other murders detailed in the detective's folder she gave me, I could find a correlation between the cultists' rituals and each attack.

Placing one hand on the boulder's craggy surface, I raised my staff and nodded to Emilie. "I'm ready when you are."

She tucked the violin under her chin and played, the haunting notes ringing out through the quiet forest. I closed my eyes, sensing the tendrils of her spellweaving intertwining with the tree's natural magic. The stone grew warm under my palm as images took shape in my mind's eye.

I saw the cultists gathered around the tree, cloaked and chanting. I heard echoes of their cryptic incantations. I watched as they wove an intricate spell, darkness amassing around the gateway.

Then a man stepped forth, crimson robes billowing as he traced an arcane symbol in the air. But the symbol didn't leave a trace of magic behind that I could examine. The next thing I knew, with a force like a punch in the face, I was jarred out of the vision.

"Damn it! Did you guys see that?"

Emilie nodded. Merlin did, too. "What butt heads!" Merlin piped up, rubbing his forehead. "That hurt. They kicked us out of there!"

I nodded. "Butt heads, indeed."

Emilie sighed and shook her head. "Don't encourage him. And watch your language in front of the boy."

I shrugged. I'd heard Emilie say "shit" dozens of times in front of Merlin. It was her favorite word. Based on the tone of her voice, though, I decided it best to simply apologize rather than challenge her credibility. A lesson learned after a decade of marriage. "Sorry. I shouldn't have said damn it. I meant *dag gummit!*"

Emilie rolled her eyes. "And butt heads?"

"What? You mean to tell me those guys *aren't* butt heads?"

Emile smirked. "Not the point, dear."

I chuckled and turned my attention back to the stone. "Clearly, they don't want us seeing what they did here. Did either of you get a good look at the symbol on their robes?"

I trailed off as Merlin retrieved his "Big Chief" tablet and a charcoal pencil from his backpack. He sat in the grass, crossed his legs, and drew.

Emilie and I stepped up behind him and examined his sketch as it came together. "That's it!" I exclaimed. "Every detail."

Merlin nodded. "It's connected to their magic. Didn't you see the symbol in the air over the tree? Just before they booted us from the vision?"

Emilie and I exchanged glances. "We didn't."

"It was the same symbol," Merlin said. "It's all connected somehow."

"Merlin, that's brilliant!" I clapped him on the shoulder. "Now we just have to figure out what it means."

Emilie peered at the image, then lifted her violin again. "I might be able to use this to focus my magic. Interact with the pattern itself. Now that we have the pattern, we should be able to get past whatever energy disrupted the vision before."

She resumed playing, and the notes vibrated through the air. The symbol glowed faintly, as if responding to her melodic spell.

I tensed, gripping my staff and placing my opposite hand back on the stone. If we could unravel the significance of this sigil, it might finally give us a lead on who these cultists were and what they wanted with the gateway.

Emilie's music swelled, and the surrounding air shimmered. The symbol from Merlin's tablet appeared as a glowing three-dimensional projection, rotating slowly. As it turned, I could see it was more complex than I first thought. Where the circles intersected a peculiar glow emerged.

The projected symbol began interacting with the shimmering air, like plugs fitting into sockets. Some kind of magical grid appeared in mid-air around us. Like a giant piece of translucent graph paper laid over everything.

"It's working!" Merlin whispered excitedly.

Abruptly, ghostly figures flickered into view within the grid. The cultists! There they were, gathered around the gateway tree again, shrouded in their crimson robes.

As one, they chanted in an eerie, unknown language. Their hoods shifted, and I saw flashes of inhuman visages—animal heads like those of the Egyptian gods. Then those too flickered, the robes too, revealing ordinary human faces and three-piece suits.

It was like these men, whoever they were, had taken off from a stockholder's meeting to go perform a murderous ritual in the park.

Who the hell were these guys?

Magic crackled through the pattern web as the cultists' chanting reached a fever pitch. Dark energy snaked around the symbol, the tendrils of ichor flowing between each robed figure and the intersections of circles within their sigil. Almost like their symbol was some kind of portal, drawing dark energy from whatever dark realm my tree connected to and charging up each cultist with nasty.

"Stand down!" a voice echoed from a distance. I turned and saw... myself. It took me by surprise. Whenever you find yourself looking at yourself... well... it can be jarring. I almost didn't recognize my voice if only because no one sounds the same as they think they do in their own head. We were seeing what happened a few hours ago, before my encounter with the cops.

"Do not interfere, Druid! This is none of your concern."

Everything happened as I'd remembered. Only now I saw more of their magic at work. This wasn't dark chaos. It was intricate, organized, magic. Not the sort of thing amateur cultists might conjure up. These people—whoever they were—knew what they were doing. They'd probably been studying their craft all their lives.

After that, it was over. The cultists dispersed in different directions, their spell complete. The vision faded away even as the cultists' dark energies receded. In seconds, the tree and the surrounding forest was back the way it was supposed to be.

Emilie lowered her violin, looking troubled. "I don't understand. Who are they?"

I shook my head. "I don't know. But I think we just glimpsed the tip of something very big and very dangerous. I should consult my father's memory. Perhaps he'll recognize what we're facing."

8. Lithomancy

THE VISION CAST BY my father's sigil stone started the same as always—I stood in the center of the ancient grove, surrounded by towering standing stones and a massive oak at its heart. The sky above shimmered with unearthly light, not quite real, but close enough to fool my senses.

I took a deep breath, steadying myself. This was no mere daydream or flight of fancy. The sigil stone in my hand connected my mind to an imprint of my father, a copy of his memories and personality captured at the moment of his death. It was him, or at least as close as magic could recreate.

I knew Em was waiting in the driver's seat of our truck, watching for trouble while I communed with Dad's ghost. Probably bored out of her skull, wishing she could join us. But the stone's magic kept me locked in a trance, and given the dangers we were facing recently, one of us needed to stay on the look-out. It was safer for everyone if I tackled this solo.

A form coalesced beside me, becoming the spitting image of my late father, Diarmid. Though not truly him, the sigil stone had copied his appearance flawlessly.

"Dad, we've got big trouble," I said.

I explained everything—the robed cultists I'd seen in the woods, the strange symbol they'd cast into the air, the way they'd manipulated the ancient tree connecting our world to others. He listened patiently, brow furrowed.

When I finished, Dad let out a long sigh.

"I cannot say who these men are," he said, "but the sorcery you describe is ancient indeed. Tell me more of their magic, son. I will explain what I can."

I nodded, trusting his wisdom even if he was just an echo. "Their power felt old, primal. I tried to stop them, but it was like they were immune to my magic."

Dad traced his fingers across the bark of the tree at the center of the grove. It wasn't an actual tree—just the memory of one, like the rest of this vision scape. "The ancients saw more than we credit them for. They knew existence was built on hidden patterns—as modern science confirms. Snowflakes, crystals... the microscopic level teems with sacred geometry. The ancients believed this was the language of the Gods, the very blueprint of creation."

"The grid those men manipulated—it's like the fabric of space and time itself. Einstein knew it, as did the ancients."

I frowned. "So, what's the significance of this? Why would anyone want to mess with something so fundamental?"

"I cannot say what their agenda is," Dad said. "But throughout history, there have been those who sought to control the sacred grid. The Druids knew of it, as did masters in the Far East and ancient Egypt. The Egyptians called it the Net—they worshipped 'Netters' who shaped reality through it. In modern times, some tried to tap this power for themselves. They specifically sought places in the world where the veil between worlds is thin and used those gateways to draw destructive energies into the world."

I tilted my head. "Which might be why they're performing their ritual around the tree in Forest Park. It's connected to Annwn."

My father nodded. "Or it was at one time. If there's no gatekeeper to guard the portal, it wouldn't take much natural ability to reconnect the tree to a different realm.

The most likely culprits belong to a school of thought known as the Weavers."

My chest tightened. "The Weavers. So these cultists... they're connected to Egyptian religion?"

Dad pursed his lips. "Yes and no. Many of the methods they use come from ancient Egypt, but they're eclectic. They use a variety of rituals and practices from a variety of secret traditions."

I shook my head. "It's like exploiting nature for human ends with no reverence for larger realities, for its beauty. As if the natural world exists to serve our warped ideas about progress and prosperity."

"If they truly can manipulate the grid at will, there's no telling what chaos might follow." At this point my father was pacing between the standing stones on each side of the grove. It was all I could do to keep up with him. "You must understand, the sages and wise men of old revered the grid. They understood how to benefit from the fabric of reality. They *bent* the grid, but never tried to change it fundamentally. The Weavers are more like children who, having learned that they can tear apart a computer to tinker with it to achieve a desired result. They don't know what they're doing. Chances are they damage the interface through their experimentation."

I frowned, trying to wrap my head around it. "So, these cultists—they're manipulating a divine blueprint of reality?"

My father nodded. "Something like that."

"But what kind of god are they dealing with? Are they connecting with one god, or many? Monotheism, or polytheism?"

Dad laughed. "Those are human concepts, Elijah. If the Divine Source is infinite, it transcends such limited categories. The Divine Source is both a unity and a plurality. Monotheists focus on the unity of divinity because the idea of competing deities is too frightening. No one wants to be collateral damage of petty squabbles between gods. But no single divine 'person,' at least insofar as we think about what a 'person' entails, can encompass the infinite. Those who worship many gods simply try to respect divinity's many aspects. Even if they conceive of their deities as multiple gods, it's still the same Divine Source that monotheists pursue. Both views are limited, and both contain truth."

"Well that just doesn't make sense. How can someone say 'there's only one God' and not be at odds with someone who reveres many gods?"

He smiled wryly. "Your Western world wants to explain everything and doubts what it can't comprehend. There's only a conflict here in your mind because you refuse to allow a notion of Divine Source that's greater than the limitations of the human mind. Think about it. If you could fully understand the Divine, it wouldn't be Divine at all. The surest sign that you're worshiping an idol of human invention is that your God concept makes too much sense."

"You're suggesting that we should pursue something absurd?"

"Not at all! I'm saying that any attempt to define Deity fully and completely is absurd by definition. The ancients were more comfortable with mystery. They *honored* mystery and resisted the urge to investigate and domesticate it."

I sighed, rubbing my temples. "This is making my head hurt."

"What's important is that these Weavers must be stopped. I cannot say if the murders littering the wake of their rituals are a part of their design or an unintended consequence."

"They sent a monster after my Merlin! Why are they attacking my son?"

"Perhaps they've come to see him as a threat. Then again, maybe it was by coincidence. The shire is a place of intense divine energy. If these cultists are manipulating energy drawn through the tree in the park, like attracts like. Perhaps they weren't seeking you so much as they were drawn to the energy of the place surrounding the shire."

I shook my head. "It felt more malevolent than that."

My father stopped pacing, faced me, and grabbed my shoulders. "I cannot tell you if that's the case because my insight is limited to the memories I had at the moment of my death. Know only this. When the Weavers have acted in modern history, the travesties that followed far exceeded whatever benefit they hoped to achieve."

I tilted my head. "Like what?"

My father pinched his chin. "The Weavers of the Twentieth Century were, in part, responsible for both World Wars. The advent of nuclear weaponry was no accident."

I shuddered. "You're saying the Nazis were Weavers?"

My father shook his head. "I'm saying that the Nazis worked with a sect of Weavers. The Weavers are not a unified community. There are different cloisters, different cohorts with independent agendas. The Manhattan Project also involved Weavers."

"That was a while ago. What have they been doing since?"

"They nearly destroyed the O-Zone in the eighties." My father licked his lips. "It wasn't all on account of hairspray. Then, there was the boy band movement in the early 2000s. I didn't live long enough to see how that panned out, but it couldn't have amounted to anything good."

I chuckled. "You're seriously blaming the Weavers for boy bands?"

My father shrugged. "How else would you explain that travesty?"

I laughed again, then my smile faded. "But people are still dying. What if the Weavers are behind the recent attacks?"

My father's expression turned grave. "It's possible. Perhaps those victims posed a threat. Or their deaths are just collateral damage, the fallout of the Weavers' machinations."

I clenched my fists. "There must be something we can do. Some way to stop them."

"Your magic taps into nature. Nature is a part of the grid, its existence. Your task is that of druids of every age—to maintain the balance, to protect the architecture of the wild. When you confront these Weavers, they're already hacked into the grid. They're manipulating reality and your magic is thwarted because it's connecting to their altered fabric. To overpower them, you must master the source. Fortify your connection to the grid. You must figure out exactly how they're manipulating it and repair what's broken."

I met his eyes. "How?"

"Seek the Sacred Grove, where your power awakens. The groves of the real world, but also the Grove of your mind's eye. Immerse yourself in its currents. Let the light of your soul fuse with its light."

I squinted. "I'm not entirely sure what that means. I've engaged nature for years. I honor the wheel of the year and the spirits of a place. What more can I do?"

"Your staff is a needle protecting the tapestry of life. But you wield your staff more like a bludgeon. It's served you well because you've never faced a threat that can alter the grid at the level of the Weavers. What this task requires is more precision, and less *boom* and *pow*."

I shook my head. "I still don't know what that means. I can do what I can do. Don't you have some kind of practical advice I can implement to battle the Weavers head-on?"

"You *must* learn their agenda. What is it they're attempting to accomplish? A physician cannot heal a disease without a diagnosis. A repairman cannot fix what's broken until he's identified the problem. Start there. Discern the agenda. Then open your mind to the surrounding spirits. The answer will show itself to you in time."

I huffed. "That's the problem. I don't even know where to start!"

"Certainly there's a clue. Something you saw that might give you a direction to pursue."

I snorted. "They were wearing suits beneath their robes. I saw as much when the vision flickered in and out of resonance."

"Then these men have worldly connections. They likely have *worldly* ends. If I were you, I'd get myself a copy of the Wall Street Journal."

I chuckled. "No one reads newspapers anymore, Dad."

"What? How do people know what's going on in the world without newspapers? Surely you still have news anchors who will tell you the truth."

I stared at my father blankly. There was no point trying to explain the current status of national news media. I got the general idea. "So look for anything on the news that might be unusual."

My father furrowed his brow. "I'd suggest exploring anything remarkable that might align with these Weavers' interests. It likely has something to do with the accumulation of wealth or power. And since you know the Weavers are operating in St. Louis, you need to find individuals with a vested interest in the accumulation of such wealth or power whose names are listed in your local phone book."

I snickered. "Right. The newspaper and the phone book. I'll do that, Dad."

9. Custard's Last Stand

I JERKED AWAKE TO find myself strapped into the passenger seat of my truck. Emilie was behind the wheel, driving aimlessly through the city streets while Merlin sat in the backseat, his curly head bent over his sketchpad as his hand flew across the page.

"The Weavers," I said. Emilie glanced at me, one eyebrow raised. "My father thinks whoever sent that shadow creature is part of a group called the Weavers. Some kind of secret society trying to rewrite reality to suit themselves."

Emilie's hands tightened on the steering wheel. "How does that explain why they're after our son?"

"I'm not sure." I ran a hand through my hair, thinking fast. "Dad's knowledge is limited. But he seemed to think the shadow was drawn to us by the ambient magic around our land, not Merlin specifically."

"That makes no sense." Emilie's voice was sharp. "There's obviously a connection with Merlin and those freaky drawings of his."

I winced. Yeah, probably should have mentioned those to Dad. "You're right, dear. I'm sorry." I let out a rueful chuckle. "Should've given me a list of questions before I went in there."

Emilie's lips quirked. "You *complain* every time I make you lists."

I stared at Emilie blankly. "Because no one likes honey-dos. But I'd rather have a list than be grilled about everything I forgot. Like I can't do a damn thing right."

Emilie tilted her head. "Whoa, buddy. Where's this coming from?"

I sighed. "Sorry. It's just this whole situation. My dad said the Weavers caused the World Wars. They saw the entire world and thousands of lives as acceptable collateral damage for whatever bullshit they were pursuing back then. But there were other Weavers played a part in building the goddamn atom bomb. That's the kind of threat we're dealing with."

Emilie checked the rear-view mirror. A subtle gesture to remind me that our son was in the back and I'd just dropped a few curses. Not the first time. Certainly wouldn't be the last.

Whatever.

Merlin was seeing visions of murderous monsters. If that didn't fuck him up, hearing me use colorful language wouldn't make any difference.

But she said nothing about that.

"This isn't your burden to carry."

"Who else is going to do it? I have to solve this!" I spoke louder than I'd intended. I took a deep breath in a futile attempt to calm down. "There's literally no one else who can stop the Weavers. But I don't even know if I can protect..." I was about to say 'our son,' but stopped myself. The last thing I needed was to cause Merlin to think I had doubts about protecting him.

Emilie reached over and took my hand. "I'm trying to tell you we're in this *together*. Let me shoulder some of the burden."

I took a deep breath and turned to stare out the passenger window. "I'll ask Dad about Merlin's drawing later. I can't risk using the stone again right away. Don't want to burn out Dad's imprint." I leaned my head back against the seat, gazing out at the city sliding past. "Whoever these

Weavers are, they're after power. We need to look for anyone who's come into money or influence recently."

Emilie snorted. "Let me guess, your dad suggested checking the newspapers?"

"Of course he did," I grinned widely. "But we have that new-fangled technology he never did. What do they call it again? The Interwebs?"

Emilie giggled a little. "We can dial up AOL and find out whatever we want to know."

"Right!" I snickered. "Seriously, though. If we cross-check anything suspicious with people currently in St. Louis, we might sniff out a lead."

Emilie shook her head. "I hope it's that easy. But if they know we're on to them, they'll be careful about covering their tracks."

"I don't know." I shook my head. "I got the impression the cultists in the park didn't think I was an actual threat. And they've been doing this a while, before we showed up in town. Why hide what you're up to when it all relies on magic? I don't know what kind of wealth or power these men are after. But they have no reason to hide, since hardly anyone would believe the truth about what they're doing, anyway."

Emile pressed her lips together. "You can get away with murder pretty easily when the weapon is a supernatural entity that no one thinks exists."

"My thoughts exactly."

"We can check the local news on our phones," Emilie said. "But there's no guarantee anything obvious has happened. At this stage of the game, they're still setting up the dominoes. Nothing that betrays their agenda will hit the news until they start knocking them over."

"But once they do, we may be too late to stop it. Maybe what they're up to won't hit the headlines. But if we do a little digging…"

Emile nodded. "If these Weavers are as powerful as your dad seems to think, they're playing a long game here."

I rubbed my brow. "I say we find a place to settle in. We're not leaving town anytime soon. Besides, I'm starving."

"I'm driving. Mind looking for a place?"

I retrieved my phone from my pocket. After a quick glance at the St. Louis Post-Dispatch website for anything local of note, but finding nothing, I logged in to Airbnb and found a listing for a Victorian house in the Central West End. "This work?"

"Book it," Emilie said.

A few more clicks and we were set. As much as I wanted to keep chasing leads, we were running on fumes. A good night's rest would do us all good.

My stomach rumbled loudly. "I swear, I could eat a barn right now."

Merlin snickered in the back seat. "Why would anyone eat a barn? That's just weird, Dad."

"Just an expression." I twisted in my seat to grin at him. "What do you say we get some Ted Drewes?"

Merlin's face lit up. "Yeah! Ted Drewes!"

I knew that would do the trick. You can't go into St. Louis *without* a serving of some of the best custard you could find anywhere. I grew up on the stuff. I don't know their recipe, but it's so creamy in your mouth... well... I can't describe it without feeling a little naughty. It's *that* good.

My order of choice? Cookie dough concrete. Largest size available. Not great for my budding dad bod... but I'd work it off. Eventually.

Emilie cleared her throat, then winked at me. "Ted Drewes *after* dinner, children!"

I huffed and crossed my arms. "Fine. You're no fun. Anyone up for Italian?"

Emilie nodded. "To the Hill!"

I had to admit, it was nice to be back in the city where I grew up. The Hill had some of the best Italian food you could find anywhere west of the Mississippi. It wasn't a long drive from there to Ted Drewes.

With all that was going on, I was antsy to get back to work, to uncover all the secrets behind the elusive Weavers and their insidious plots. But whatever they were up to, it hadn't destroyed the world yet. More people would die, of course, if they struck again. But we'd be in no shape to deal with the situation if we didn't have some sustenance and rest.

I settled back in my seat, exhaustion settling over me but also a simmering anticipation. We had a lot of unanswered questions, but at least we had a lead. We knew more about who we were dealing with than we did just hours before. Tomorrow we'd start putting together the pieces of this puzzle. For now, it was enough that we were safe and together.

The End of Part One

INTERLUDES I

Merlin ◆ Sloane

I.1.1. Merlin

My charcoal stick raced across the page as the truck bumped down the dirt road. Dumb potholes. Hard to get all the details right like this.

Ted Drewes' custard was calling me, but so were the monsters.

I had to draw them. Maybe if I kept drawing, I'd figure out something to help Mom and Dad stop them.

The shapes flowed out of my pencil like magic. Long tentacles, sharp teeth, glowing eyes—details popped into my head as fast as I could put them on paper.

Where did these ideas come from? I didn't know, but I was sure they meant something. The monsters were trying to tell me something through my drawings.

When the Gateway Arch appeared on my page, rising from the muddy river, I knew this sketch was important. The monster was emerging from under the arch, like it had come from somewhere else. Was the Arch actually a portal? Kinda looked like one. Though a little more science-fictiony that any portal I'd ever seen.

I scrubbed my pencil faster across the paper, adding shadows and textures. The monster had to look real so Mom and Dad would understand. I couldn't hold back on any details. Anything that popped into my head. I had to get it down. They'd know what to do with this clue, even if I didn't understand it myself.

All I knew was that the monsters were coming, and we had to stop them before it was too late. My drawings were the only way I could help.

Mom and Dad were always so protective. Like I was of my stuffed dragon toy I used to cuddle with at night. Not anymore, of course. I'm ten. Ten-year-olds can't cuddle with stuffies. But "Mister Scales" had seen me through some hard years. Growing up ain't easy, you know. Especially when your dad is some kind of super cool druid and... you know... they had such high expectations of me.

"Some day," Dad often said, "you'll be even more powerful than me. You're going to do amazing things, Merlin."

Whatever. I'm not dumb. He was my dad. Of course he'd think that. He was a little biased, you know. I had to wonder—did every dad think his son was going to save the world some day?

A lot to live up to. But, hey. I guess I'd rather my parents have big dreams for me than crappy ones. I didn't want to end up flipping burgers for a living. So why not be a kick butt druid like Dad? I mean, not nearly as cool as becoming a YouTuber. But I could do worse.

"Whatcha working on there, bud?" my dad asked, peering over from the front seat.

I hesitated. I knew he'd freak out. They were so worried about my drawings before. But I had to show him. Slowly, I turned my sketchpad around.

Dad's eyes went wide. His face turned pale. I had drawn a massive shadow monster—like the one who attacked us before, but way bigger—rising from the muddy Mississippi near the Arch, its jaws open wide, rows of razor-sharp teeth glinting. A man ran screaming as it swiped at him with dagger-like claws.

"Merlin..." Dad said quietly. "This is very concerning. Where is this coming from?"

I shrugged, staring down at my lap. "I dunno. The pictures just come to me. I can't control it."

Dad took a deep breath. His lips made a mouth fart as he exhaled. "I know you want to help, son. But until we understand these premonitions more, it's best to not dwell on such darkness. Let's just try to enjoy a nice dinner and Ted Drewes, okay?"

I nodded, but inside I was frustrated. Why couldn't Dad see? These weren't just random doodles. They were warnings. Signs of what could come if we didn't figure out how to stop it. But how could we stop what we didn't understand? I had to keep digging into the shadows of my strange mind, no matter how scary, to find the answers.

Mom glanced at me in the rear-view mirror. "Sweetie, I know you're trying to make sense of all this. But we have to be smart. Drawing these creatures over and over will only strengthen their hold on you."

I frowned. They didn't get it. This wasn't about me. People were in danger. "But Mom, what if I can help? What if there's some clue in my pictures that could stop the monsters for good?"

Mom sighed, her eyes filled with sympathy and concern. "I understand, Merlin. But you're just a boy. This burden isn't yours to bear alone."

I crossed my arms, staring defiantly out the window. It wasn't fair. Grownups always thought they knew best, but they didn't know everything. My drawings flowed from some deep well inside me I didn't understand. But I knew if I could tap into it more, unravel its mysteries, I could unlock secrets to defeat the gathering darkness.

Mom and Dad meant well, but they underestimated me. I wouldn't stop searching for answers, no matter what they said. The monsters had to be stopped. And if I could help do that by peering into the shadows of my mind, then so be it. I wasn't just a boy. I was Merlin. And one day, if I couldn't have my own YouTube channel, I'd be more powerful than they were. Don't blame me for my ego. They were the ones who put that idea in my head to begin with. They told me I was destined for greatness. Why not start now?

I.2.3. Sloane

The squad car's tires squealed as we took the corner, siren wailing into the night. My fingers drummed anxiously on the armrest while Ernie leaned over the wheel, foot heavy on the gas.

"Keep it together, Harding," I muttered under my breath. Ever since that thing in the park, I'd been on edge. Monsters weren't real. Magic wasn't real. But I'd seen it with my own eyes. That man—Elijah Wadsworth—had done the impossible.

"What's that, Sloane?" Ernie grunted, not bothering to look my way. "You say something?"

"Just drive," I snapped back. Couldn't let him see me shaken. Ernie was always looking for signs of weakness, something to leverage himself higher in the department. If he got the slightest hint I was out of my right mind, if I mentioned shadow monsters and strange wizards in the park, he'd have me in the chief's office faster than you could say, "paid leave" and "mandatory therapy."

Ernie wasn't the kind of guy I'd choose as a partner. But when you're inadequately funded, understaffed, and you're policing a city with some of the highest crime rates in the country, beggars can't be choosers.

Ernie was a good cop, mostly. A little too ambitious. Like a lot of men on the force who'd never admit as much, he didn't take female officers seriously. It didn't matter that I outranked him. He *always* thought he knew better. Like I'd only been promoted because I was a woman—because it was "politically expedient" for the chief to put women in positions of authority.

It didn't help that I was ten years Ernie's junior.

Thing was, I'd worked twice as hard to get to my position as any of the other detectives on the force. I graduated at the top of my class—both for my *degree* in Criminal Justice *and* at the Academy. Ernie didn't go to school for detective work at all. Nothing against rising the ranks through the traditional route. That's why it took him so much longer to get to where he was. Some of the best detectives I knew didn't have college degrees.

Either way, I'd *earned* my place. And I'd solved some really tough cases as of late. Until I'd encountered... whatever that nightmare was in the park... this latest string of homicides had me (and the rest of the department) baffled.

How was I supposed to solve this *now* without looking like I was more suited for a straight jacket than the uniform?

That's the thing about being a woman on the force. There's no room for error. There's always some *dick* in the department (because that's what they used to call detectives, you know) looking to stick it to me. Literally *and* figuratively.

Enough complaining. I knew what I was getting into when I chose this career. But every now and again, I'd be lying if I didn't admit that it got under my skin.

I was damn good at my job and no one *else* questioned it. Except for every goddamn man who'd been assigned as my partner over the last three years.

We screeched to a halt at the scene, blue and red lights painting the dark riverbank. Two beat cops stood waiting, hands on their belts. I stepped out, gravel crunching under my boots.

Ernie lumbered out a second later, adjusting his belt. "Detectives Harding and Thompson. What have we got?"

The taller cop jerked his chin toward the body lying half in the mud, half in the water. "Homeless guy. No ID yet. Probably an overdose."

I narrowed my eyes, scanning the scene. The ground was disturbed, boot prints tracking through the dirt. It looked like someone dragged him to where he was. But there was no second set of footprints. No blood or readily visible wounds.

"You're sure about that?" I asked.

The cop shrugged. "That's what it looks like to me."

I walked the perimeter of the scene. The hairs on the back of my neck prickled. Nine times out of ten when a homeless person is involved, the investigators on-scene rush to "overdose" as the likely cause of death.

I don't care how high or intoxicated someone might be. You can't drag your own body across the dirt like that. Someone either covered their tracks well or this was another victim of the weird.

I stood, dusting off my hands. "Get CSU down here to process the scene. This is connected to the others."

Ernie looked up from his examination, brows drawing together. "What are you talking about? There's no sign of foul play."

"Gut feeling," I said shortly. "This man was dragged here. Usually, I'd assume the killer covered their tracks. But given what we've been dealing with lately… whatever… we can't be too cautious. Just get CSU on it. Now."

Ernie opened his mouth to argue but seemed to think better of it. If I was deploying department resources to investigate a simple overdose, well, he was willing to allow me to fall on my own proverbial sword. But I wasn't wrong about this. Then again, what would CSU be able to prove if my suspicions were correct? We weren't dealing with a regular killer.

I walked to the water's edge, staring out at the rolling surface of the river. The same uneasy feeling I'd had in the park was back, prickling at my senses. Something wasn't right in St. Louis, and this was only the beginning.

The question was, did I want to know how deep this rabbit hole went?

What choice did I have? I needed to solve these cases. But I would not do it alone. It wasn't often that I was in over my head. I had to play this one close to the chest.

Conspiring with someone who was barely *not* a suspect wouldn't bode well for me in the long run. But I knew Wadsworth wasn't guilty. He'd saved my life. And if he knew anything that could help identify the actual killer, I needed him.

PART II

The Cultists' Sigil

10. The Naked Truth

The grand Victorian mansion loomed before us, all spires and turrets and ornate scrollwork. Emilie's eyes went wide as saucers. My stomach was turning from eating too much. I *almost* regretted the extra-large cookie dough concrete.

"It's gorgeous!" Emilie breathed. "We should buy this place instead of just renting it."

I laughed. "What's wrong with the shire?"

"Nothing," Emilie said. "But wouldn't it be nice to have a pied-à-terre in the city? I love our little corner of the Ozarks as much as you do, but you have to admit, a change of pace now and then would be nice."

"The pace of the city isn't exactly relaxing," I pointed out.

"Relaxation isn't always the point," she countered. "It might be good to live closer to other people. I know we're homeschooling Merlin, and his abilities make that the right call. But we could connect with other homeschool families here in the city. He needs more social interaction."

I tilted my head. "He gets plenty of social interaction."

Emilie stared at me blankly. "The squirrels don't count."

"That's not fair." I did my best to suppress my laughter. "We have rabbits and deer, too."

"He needs friends, Elijah. Why do you think he's glued to that tablet all the time?"

I had to laugh again. No point holding it back. She had a point. Our little warlock could use some friends his own age. When this mess with the Weavers was over, maybe a second home in the city wasn't such a bad idea. If the owners were willing to sell, I could easily afford it. Thanks to some wise investments made by an older version of my time-traveling son, I had more money than I knew what to do with.

I wasn't sure if the advantages of time-travel constituted insider trading, but what was the SEC going to do about it?

In a round-about way, Merlin provided for all of us. Even if the boy I was raising wouldn't set that up until he was much older.

MERLIN'S MANTLE

Emilie grinned, knowing she'd made her point. Hook, line and sinker. That's my girl. Always two steps ahead. God, I loved her.

We headed inside, ready to settle in. But knowing our Merlin, this stately manor was sure to get a lot less stately before our stay was through. The kid was a walking hurricane of chaos. But he was *our* hurricane.

If only he learned the "cleaning" spell that Merlin used to help "the Wart" out with his chores in Disney's *Sword and the Stone*. Though, I suspected the writers of that cartoon took a few artistic liberties. Because the Merlin I knew had the cleanliness skills of a dung beetle.

I couldn't help but chuckle as Merlin immediately took off, racing from room to room. He was like a pinball, ricocheting off the antique furnishings.

"Careful, buddy!" I called after him. But it was useless. That kid didn't have a careful bone in his body.

He slid to a stop in front of a marble sculpture of a nude woman, his eyes widening. Ah jeez. I probably should have anticipated this. Most prepubescent boys weren't confronted with fine Renaissance art on a daily basis.

"Merlin, look away please," Emilie gently chided.

"But Mom! It's so...so...pretty!" he exclaimed, his eyes glued to the statue.

"Yes, art is wonderful," I said. "But let's keep moving and find your room, okay?"

"Aww, come on Dad!" Merlin whined. "How come? You always say it's important to appreciate women."

Emilie stifled a laugh. "He's got you there," she said, giving me a wry smile.

I just shook my head, grinning. The kid was too damn clever for his own good. But that was our Merlin. Chaos and cleverness all rolled into one lanky package.

After we finally got Merlin tucked into the room next door, Emilie and I retreated to the master suite. The moment the door closed behind us, I pulled Emilie into my arms.

It had been far too long. Between chasing down leads on this case and homeschooling Merlin, we hadn't had a moment to ourselves in ages.

Emilie melted against me with a contented sigh, her hands sliding up my chest. I dipped my head and captured her lips, the familiar warmth and softness making my heart stutter.

We'd been together for over a decade, but Emilie still had the power to make me feel like a love-struck teenager. I deepened the kiss, my hands roaming over the curves I knew by heart.

A low moan rumbled in Emilie's throat, spurring me on. I slid my hands under her shirt, skimming the smooth skin of her back.

Just then, the Westminster chimes echoed through the house. We jumped apart, chests heaving.

"Damn it!" I growled. "Who's ringing the doorbell at this time of night?"

My heart was still pounding, but not from desire anymore. Who on earth would show up unannounced at nearly midnight? At an Airbnb no less? This couldn't be good.

With a resigned sigh, I straightened my clothes and headed downstairs to the front door. Peering through the peephole, I blinked in surprise. Detective Harding stared back at me, her expression grim.

Shit. I turned back to Emilie, who had followed me down the stairs. "It's that goddamn detective. How the hell did she know where to find us?"

Emilie frowned, worry etched on her brow. "I don't know," she mumbled. "She is a detective, you know."

"Yeah. No shit, Sherlock." I shook my head, frustrated that we couldn't get a moment alone without having to deal with... all this shit. "Bad detective joke. Sorry."

Emilie shrugged, though her eyes were still troubled. "You should open the door. Find out what she wants."

I released an exacerbated sigh before turning the knob. Detective Harding stood on the porch, hands on her hips.

"Hello Mr. Wadsworth," she said, smirking. "Got a minute? This goddamn detective has a few questions for you."

I winced, realizing she'd overheard my less-than-flattering remark. "You heard that, huh? Sorry about that."

Harding laughed dryly. "No offense taken. Mind if I come in?"

I stepped back reluctantly, allowing her inside. Emilie hovered nearby, arms folded over her chest.

Harding's smirk vanished as she met my gaze. "There's been another body. This time by the river."

Emilie and I exchanged glances, alarm rising. Merlin's latest drawing—the shadow monster lurking by the Mississippi.

"Was it near the arch?" I asked tersely.

Harding's eyes narrowed. "Yes, it was. How'd you know?"

I scrambled for a plausible excuse. "Lucky guess. The riverfront's not that big downtown. Had to be somewhere around there."

Harding studied me for a long moment before continuing. "This killing isn't like the others. No strange wounds, no discernible cause of death. Though we won't know for sure until the autopsy comes back. Still, just like the others, no leads." She fixed me with an intense stare. "My partner doesn't think the same perp is behind it. They're saying overdose. They might be right. But my instincts tell me it's connected."

My pulse spiked, but I kept my face carefully blank. "I wish I could help you, Detective. But I'm as stumped as you are."

Harding clearly wasn't buying it. This wasn't over. Not by a long shot.

Harding's eyes bored into mine, as if trying to extract the truth through sheer force of will. "Let me be frank, Mr. Wadsworth. I know there's more going on here than meets the eye. These killings have an uncanny pattern."

"I thought you said this one differed from the others," I piped in.

"What's common to these cases is that there's always something about them I can't explain. Something that defies logic. I'm good at my job, Mr. Wadsworth. I've solved a lot of cases. Rarely am I this stumped. But each one of these cases as of late has proven more elusive than the last. That *is* the pattern."

She paused, lowering her voice. "You said something about 'cultists' last time. Was that just a load of bullshit or do you know more that you're letting on about who might be behind this?"

I hesitated, warring with myself. How much could I reveal without putting more people at risk? My family was already a target. But if Harding or anyone else from the department went after these people… things could get bloody, fast. But she *was* coming to me for help.

"I don't have any names," I said finally. "I'll tell you what you want know if you promise me to be careful. Don't go after these people without looping me in."

"Mr. Wadsworth, I can't bring a civilian with no… credible expertise in on a case. I'd never be able to get it approved."

"Then tell them you think I'm a witness. That I might identify who is involved. I saw things in the park, you know."

Harding shook her head. "A line up might work. But we can't do that unless we have cause to arrest someone."

"I'm not telling you anything unless you bring me along. This isn't a joke, Detective. These people are dangerous in ways you aren't prepared for. You saw that monster in the park. You know I'm telling you the truth."

Harding pinched her chin. "Fine. I'll figure something out. You have a deal."

I nodded. "Alright. I consulted with a... mentor of mine. Have you ever heard of a group called the Weavers?"

Harding's eyes narrowed, processing this. "The Weavers," she repeated. "Can't say I've come across them before. Any idea what they're about?"

I shook my head. "They could be using a religious organization as cover, perhaps some kind of philosophical society. All I know is that powerful men are involved."

"Businessmen?" Harding cocked an eyebrow. "Politicians?"

"Probably. Could be lawyers, stockbrokers, whatever. I don't know. All I can say is that they're men of means."

Harding paled slightly, but her jaw tightened with resolve. "I'll look into these Weavers. I have a lot of connections. In the meantime, if you hear anything more…"

Just then, a small voice piped up from the doorway.

"Dad? What's going on?"

I turned to see Merlin rubbing his eyes, clutching his stuffed dragon. He didn't sleep with it back home, but we were in a strange house. At ten, you can still get away with a few childish habits and no one will hold it against you. All I could figure was that the doorbell woke him up. There was no telling how long he'd been standing there listening in.

"Nothing to worry about," I said gently. "Detective Harding just had some questions. You should be in bed."

But Merlin was already wandering over, curiosity sparking his gaze. "Hey, you're the lady who arrested Dad today!"

Harding gave a wry smile. "Yes, that was me. But it was just a misunderstanding. I'm not here to arrest your father." She crouched down to Merlin's level. "But your parents are right. This is adult stuff. You shouldn't concern yourself with it."

Merlin's eyes went wide. "But I can help!"

Emilie shot me a worried look. Neither of us was thrilled about exposing our son to this macabre business. But before we could intervene, Merlin was already digging a folded paper out of his pajamas.

"I drew a picture earlier. After we left the police station," he explained eagerly. "Here. I have more like it if it helps."

He handed Harding the paper. Her eyes bugged as she unfolded it, taking in the expertly rendered scene—the shadowy figure, the victim, the riverside backdrop.

"How did you draw this?" she demanded hoarsely. "That's exactly what I saw tonight. The details..."

Merlin shrugged, suddenly shy. "I just saw it in my head. And I can draw really well. That's my gift." He peeked up at Harding. "It helps, right?"

Harding looked between us, questions burning in her eyes. But she simply folded the drawing and slipped it into her pocket.

Harding took a deep breath, composing herself. "Merlin, you have an incredible talent. This drawing...it's going to help a lot."

She paused, weighing her next words. "Did you say you have other pictures like this? Ones that might give me more clues about the... the shadowy figure?"

Merlin's face lit up. "Yeah, lots!" He glanced at Emilie and me, suddenly hesitant. "Can I show her?"

Emilie and I exchanged a look. Neither of us were thrilled about exposing our son further to any of this. But if it helped the investigation...

Emilie nodded slowly. "It's okay, sweetheart. Go ahead."

"Be right back!" Merlin cried, already dashing off.

Harding watched him go, shaking her head in wonderment. "How does he do it? The detail, the accuracy...it's unbelievable."

I shrugged, feigning nonchalance even as my guts twisted. "He's always had a knack for art. And a wild imagination."

Harding frowned. "This is beyond imagination, Mr. Wadsworth. This is a window into things unseen. Things..." she trailed off, lost in thought.

Footsteps pounded down the hall. Merlin skidded back into the room, clutching his drawing pad.

"Got it!" He presented the pad to Harding with a flourish. "My Big Chief tablet. All my best pictures are in here."

Harding took it carefully, almost reverently. She sank onto the sofa, engrossed as she slowly turned each page.

We hovered nearby, tense. I wasn't sure if showing her was the right call. But the die was cast now. All we could do was hope Merlin's drawings provided more answers than questions.

11. Tainted Proof

THE GLOW OF THE lamp cast shadows across the detective's face, accentuating the bags under her eyes as she rifled through a folder of crime scene photos. She picked one up, squinting at it, then placed it carefully in Merlin's drawing pad atop the matching sketch.

"What are you doing?" I asked.

"Making connections," she murmured. Her eyes darted rapidly between the photos and drawings. "This is incredible. There's a sketch in here for every single one of my unsolved cases."

I leaned in for a closer look. She was right. Merlin had captured details that neither Emilie nor I imagined were the least bit significant. But the detective was clearly making connections we couldn't.

Harding let out a low whistle. "Even the Barlow case. Rogers refused to believe it was a homicide. Wasn't my case, so there wasn't anything I could do. This proves it, though."

"Proves it?" I raised my left eyebrow.

Harding's shoulders rose and fell. "Well, not the kind of proof a prosecutor would need. But saying I believe all of this... whatever it is you people do is real. This proves to *me* that I'm right. It points me in the right direction and spares me from pursuing dead-end theories. If I can work backwards and find evidence I can use..."

"So you believe in our abilities?" I asked. "I know you saw me take down that monster. It's one thing to see it but, in my experience, seeing isn't always believing. People will go to any length to *dismiss* the supernatural, even if it's staring them in the face."

"Why would someone ignore the obvious?" Harding asked.

I bit my lip. "It's easier to think you're seeing things, that maybe you were momentarily crazy, in order to maintain their narrow worldview, than to admit that things like magic, witches and druids, monsters, vampires and werewolves...."

Harding dropped everything and stared at me blankly. "Vampires and werewolves? What the hell else is out there I never knew about?"

Emilie chuckled. "More than even we understand. But suffice it to say, if you've read about it, or saw Sam and Dean Winchester take it down on television, there's a good chance there's *something* similar to it in the real world."

Harding nodded. "I don't know about any of that. With this case, though? I certainly believe there's something *beyond* the normal going on. You told me earlier that your family just arrived in the city earlier today."

I nodded. "That's right. Haven't been in town for months."

"This case," Harding picked up one of Merlin's drawings in one hand and a crime-scene photo in the other. "It was three weeks ago. There *is* no other way to explain it."

I grinned. "Do you believe in magic?"

Emilie groaned. "Please don't start singing, Elijah."

"I'm beginning to believe, for sure," Harding added before I could respond to Emilie's remark with a few bars from the Lovin' Spoonful song. The detective's voice was full of a youthful exuberance that stood in stark contrast to the demanding tone she'd used with me when she was questioning me downtown.

I glanced at Merlin. He sat cross-legged on the floor, tongue poking out in concentration as he watched the detective's every move. He was proud of himself. And for good reason.

Harding's eyes shone with a glint that told me she was hot on the trail. "There are clues here," she muttered. "Details the killer left behind, but we either missed or were already gone before we got to the scene. If I can just put it all together…"

I opened my mouth to respond, but Harding held up a hand to stop me before I could get a word out.

"Sorry, that was rude of me," she said, not taking her eyes off the drawings and crime scene photos spread out on the coffee table. "I'm just trying to make some connections here and need to stay focused."

I nodded, clamping my mouth shut. Harding was clearly onto something big.

Meanwhile, Merlin hopped on the couch and was practically bouncing up and down with excitement. "This is so cool!" he exclaimed. "I can't believe I actually helped solve real police cases."

I put a hand on his shoulder. "Alright, kiddo, I think it's time you headed up to bed. It's late."

Merlin's eyes went wide. "What? No way! This is way too exciting. There's no way I'll be able to sleep now!"

I had to chuckle. The kid had a point. After an evening like this, I doubted any of us would get much rest tonight.

"Well, at least try to wind down a bit," I suggested. "Why don't you go grab one of your comic books or something?"

Merlin huffed dramatically but slid off the couch to head upstairs anyway, the promise of superhero adventures at least temporarily overriding his fascination with our real-life detective downstairs.

Harding barely seemed to notice Merlin's departure, still wholly engrossed in studying the contents of his sketches. Her brow was furrowed in concentration, but her eyes shone with the light of discovery. I could almost see the gears turning in her head as she pieced together connections.

"The intricacy of these sketches..." she murmured. "It's uncanny. There are details here that we never picked up on at the actual crime scenes. It's like Merlin somehow psychically tuned into exactly what was happening in the moments these murders took place."

She tapped a finger on one drawing, her eyes lighting up. "See this pattern here in the background? This matches the wallpaper in the victim's apartment." Harding traced her finger to the side. "But see this shadow? It's not the monster. The way the light is cast throughout the drawing, it doesn't fit. There's someone else there. Almost as if your son captured this image through someone else's eyes. Like Merlin is taking a snapshot of what someone actually saw. I can use this drawing to recreate the scene, go back there, and maybe pick up something that will give me a clue who was there and why."

Harding shook her head in amazement. "With clues like these, we'll be able to recreate a lot of the details about the crime scenes we missed before."

She glanced up at me, a fierce determination in her eyes. "I think we're close to a breakthrough here. Just give me a little more time with these sketches, and I know I can unravel this whole mystery."

I nodded. "It looks like Merlin may have provided the missing puzzle pieces you needed."

Harding carefully gathered up the drawings. "I'm going to need to take photos of these to study later, if that's alright. Would Merlin mind if I borrowed them temporarily?"

"I'm sure he'd be thrilled to keep helping in any way he can," I replied.

Harding's lips curved into a smile—the first real, unguarded smile I'd seen from her. "Then let's get cracking. The faster I can get these back to the station to analyze, the sooner we can catch these Weavers in the act and bring them to justice."

Her enthusiasm was contagious. With Harding on the case, we might identify the Weavers. At least we had a better chance now than we did before. Stopping them though? That was another issue entirely. When they were casting in the park, my magic didn't work. My spell *did* work on the monsters they made. That meant I just had to strike at them when they weren't prepared. If Harding could identify the cultists, I could approach them when they least expected me. Maybe I could disarm them, silence their abilities—whatever they were. There was still a lot to learn, but we were a *big* step closer than we were just an hour earlier.

Harding began snapping photographs of Merlin's drawings with her phone. As she finished, I gently placed my hand on her arm.

"Detective Harding, I know you're excited about this breakthrough, but remember—we had a deal. You agreed not to move against the Weavers without me. It's simply too perilous to confront them alone."

Harding sighed, her initial elation dimming. "You're right. Call me Sloane, by the way. Since this investigation is off the books; might as well drop the formalities."

She glanced down at my hand still resting on her arm and I quickly withdrew it. Sloane gave me a wry smile.

"Here's the thing, Elijah. Officially, you're not involved in this case. I can feed you tidbits here and there, but have to be careful how I play this. Not just for my credibility's sake, but for the sake of your family."

I nodded. "I understand. But Sloane, there's too much at stake here. More than you realize."

She raised an eyebrow. "There always is. That's why it's an *ongoing* investigation, Wadsworth."

I snorted. "Call me Elijah. But it's more than the investigations. There could be a much larger threat than murderous cultists. Especially if these are the same Weavers I've heard about."

"Go on."

"It's believed the Weavers are part of an ancient order," I explained. "One that's appeared at pivotal moments throughout history—often right before major conflicts like the world wars. They crave power and influence, no matter the cost."

Sloane's expression had grown serious as she listened. "If what you're saying is true, we need to stop them quickly. Before their schemes spiral even further out of control."

"Exactly," I agreed. "Which is why we need to work together on this. We don't just share tid-bits. We're partners a hundred percent. I will tell you everything I learn. You do the same. The Weavers won't hesitate to remove anyone who gets in their way—detective or not."

Sloane considered this for a moment before giving a resolute nod. "Alright, I'll keep you in the loop. I won't move against these people without letting you know. But what I told you before still holds. Be careful. If my superiors—or my asshole of a partner—gets wind of you sniffing around these cases, I may not be able to protect you."

I nodded resolutely. "Understood. It's agreed. I'll be careful, but you need to be, too."

Sloane glanced at her watch. "I should get going. Lots of leads to follow up on. Looks like it'll be a whole coffee pot night for me."

"Do what you need to do," I said. "But there's nothing more we can do tonight. Working magic requires me to be at my best. If I have to fight these Weavers, or any more of their monsters, I'm going to need my beauty sleep."

Emilie snickered. "His magic reflects his mood. You don't want to see Elijah when he's cranky."

Sloane winked at Emilie. "Oh, I work with a lot of men. I know how that is."

"Hey!" I added. "I'm standing right here!"

"Get some rest tonight," Sloane said. "Reach out to me *immediately* if Merlin draws anything else. If we move fast, we might catch the perps on scene."

I nodded. "Got it. I've still got your card."

Sloane nodded and headed for the door. "Good. This isn't going to be an open-and-shut case. We've got a long fight ahead of us."

With that, she was gone. Emilie ran her hand up and down my back. "Well, that went about as well as we could hope."

I nodded. "I suppose you're right."

Emilie interlaced her fingers with mine and we headed back to the master bedroom. By this time, we were too exhausted—more mentally than physically—to enjoy our alone-time.

If my mind wasn't racing too much, I doubted it would take me long to fall asleep. But that was a big *if*.

I knew working with the detective gave us the best shot we had, but there was an uneasy feeling deep in my gut. I hated how involved in all of this Merlin was—and now the cops were *depending* on him. Well, Sloane was at least.

What would her fellow officers, who *didn't* believe in magic, think if they came across his drawings of crime scenes that Merlin shouldn't have known about? Could I really trust Sloane's discretion in all of this? I didn't really know her. Our interactions had done little to give me a real barometer reading of her character.

"Are you sure we're doing the right thing?" I asked as I pulled back the blankets on the bed and swung my legs onto the mattress.

"What choice do we have?" Emilie asked as she slipped in beside me. "We aren't professional investigators, Elijah. Sloane is trained for this. I think we'll make a fine team."

I snorted. "If no one gets hurt. I mean, we're bringing her into a world that's going to open up a wide range of questions for her. Once you know the supernatural exists, it's not like you can go back to business as usual. Every case she has from here on out, she'll have a thousand other possibilities in the back of her mind that she'd never have considered before."

Emilie laughed a little. "You're seriously worried about Sloane's future career success?"

I leaned over and kissed Emilie once on the lips. "You're right. I'm just worried in general. I'm grasping at straws, trying to find the right reason why my instincts are telling me that flight would be wiser than fight right now. Like we're opening up a can of worms we won't be able to close."

Emilie kissed me back. "If we open up the can of worms, we'll just have to go fishing. One thing at a time, babe."

12. Hold your Tongue, Say Apple.

THE MORNING SUN PEEKED through the curtains, assaulting my eyes. I squinted, rolling over to see Emilie's sleeping face. She looked so peaceful, her chest rising and falling with each breath. I brushed a strand of hair from her cheek and pressed a gentle kiss there before slipping out from under the covers.

My stomach rumbled angrily as I pulled on a t-shirt. We'd been so preoccupied since arriving here, there hadn't been time to stock the kitchen.

"We're out of food," I said, my voice gravelly with sleep.

Emilie groaned, burrowing deeper into her pillow. "There's a shocker. Because we never had any."

I leaned down to give her a proper good morning kiss, morning breath be damned. She indulged me for a moment before playfully pushing me away.

"I'll run out and grab something. Pancakes sound good?"

"Mmm, sure," she murmured. "With chocolate chips?"

"As you wish." I tucked the covers around her and made my way to Merlin's room. Quiet snores greeted me as I peeked in. The kid could sleep through the apocalypse. Must get that from his mother.

My stomach gurgled again, spurring me toward the door.

I stepped outside into the cool morning air, taking a moment to appreciate the old mansion's tranquility. Most places this old had seen their fair share of tragedy, leaving residual energy that prickled my druid senses. But this home radiated calm. Love saturated its history. If we ever got a place in the city, I hoped we'd find a sanctuary like this.

I located the nearest grocery store, a Schnucks I knew from my time growing up in St. Louis, not twenty minutes from our Airbnb. The automatic doors slid open, and I grabbed a basket, my mind on pancakes and toppings. Syrup was a must. Berries too, for a pop of color.

Hell, why not load up on all the essentials? Nothing about anything we'd learned so far told me that this situation was going to have a quick resolution.

We needed some cereal, bread and milk. Snacks for Merlin. A lot of fruit. All the fixings for a salad.

I made my way to the produce section, drawn by the bright piles of apples, oranges, and bananas. As I inspected a bulbous Fuji, a man in a tailored suit sidled up beside me.

"Fine apples this season, aren't they, Mr. Wadsworth?" he remarked casually, not making eye contact.

My head snapped up.

I eyed the stranger warily. How did he know my name?

My gaze landed on a small, familiar tattoo peeking out from under his shirt cuff. The same honeycomb-like sigil I'd seen on the cloaks of the Weavers who'd attacked us. A collection of intersecting circles, identical to the one Merlin produced before.

Shit. I tensed, ready to act.

"Now, now, no need for dramatics," the man said smoothly, his focus still on the apples. "We wouldn't want to cause a scene. After all, I know exactly where your lovely wife and son are sleeping at this very moment."

Fury boiled up inside me, but I forced myself to breathe, to maintain my composure. I couldn't risk Emilie's and Merlin's safety.

"In fact, my associates could have her—and your especially intriguing boy—in hand faster than you could utter a spell," he continued. "But we'd much rather have a civilized chat."

Through clenched teeth, I asked, "What do you want?"

The man chuckled. "Why, to recruit you, of course. A man of your talents would be a valuable asset to our organization. Your son's destiny might depend on your compliance."

I narrowed my eyes. I knew from my father's memories what kind of shit the Weavers were responsible for. There was no way in the depths of hell I'd join them. Still, I wasn't going to learn anything by being an ass. And if he really did have people spying on my family...

I had no choice but to play along. It was best he think I was considering his proposal rather than escalate the confrontation. "What does any of this have to do with my son?"

"Ah yes, the boy. Let's just say we know who he is going to become. We'd prefer not to interfere with that. But Merlin's destiny is in peril, Mr. Wadsworth. He'll never don the mantle he's meant to assume if you don't join us."

I cocked an eyebrow. "Is that supposed to be a threat?"

"Not a threat. It's a fact. Horrible things are happening. All these unnecessary murders. We want them to stop as much as you do."

His words dripped with mock sincerity. I wanted to wipe that smug look off his face. I was a druid in the produce section. I was more dangerous here than a Marine in an armory.

I could use my power and sprout a hundred apple trees from the seeds in the bin. I could animate them to life and they'd rip this guy apart if I wished. Maybe I'd sprout a vine from the grapes and choke him right out.

There was a lot I *could do*. But if these assholes had eyes on my family, I couldn't risk it. I had to keep my family safe, even if it meant placating this bastard. For now.

I clenched my jaw, grinding my teeth. "You say all these 'horrible things' and 'unnecessary murders' will cease if I join you. Yet you threaten my family to get what you want. Forgive me if I find your sincerity lacking."

The man shrugged, examining an apple as if this were any normal conversation. "We only resort to such tactics when people are...uncooperative. Once you're with us, you'll understand our cause is just."

"You still haven't told me what this is all about," I said. "What is your 'cause' exactly?"

"All in due time, Mr. Wadsworth. There are certain things it would behoove neither of us to discuss in public. I've told you we intend you no ill. That doesn't mean there aren't others who do."

I shook my head. "I know that tattoo on your wrist. I saw it in the park. I also know all about the Weavers and the bullshit they've pulled through the centuries."

"We are not all alike!" the man insisted, his tone more curt than before. "Is every man who owns a firearm to blame for every murder committed with one? We practice an ancient art, I admit it. But not all Weavers are careless nor are we all concerned only with power."

I snorted. "Don't judge an ass by its stench. I get it. But even the cutest little bubble butts still drop turds from time to time."

The man tilted his head. "Your metaphors are... unusual... Mr. Wadsworth."

I shrugged. "I live with a ten-year old boy. What do you expect?"

The man handed me a small index card. "At least you have a good sense of humor about it. But I can assure you, there's nothing humorous about what will happen if you are not fully aligned with our cause by night's end."

I gulped. "Night's end? What happens tonight?"

"Be at that address half an hour from now, and come alone. We will explain everything."

I didn't like any of this. Not one bit. But I didn't have much choice. This guy had me over a barrel.

I took the card, glancing at the address scribbled on it. I didn't know exactly what building it represented, but it was downtown. Exactly where the few corporate elites who called St. Louis their headquarters did their business.

"And if I refuse?" I asked, meeting the man's gaze.

He gave me an icy smile. "I believe we've already covered the consequences of non-compliance."

My hands curled into fists again. I could feel the earth beneath my feet, the lifeforce flowing through it. So much power, so much *potential* all around me. But I couldn't do a damn thing.

Being powerless sucks. Having more power than you need but not being able to use it sucks twice as hard.

I forced myself to take a breath. "Fine. I'll meet with your people. But at least tell me your name."

The man nodded. "My name is Alessandro. I will meet you at the address on the card. Don't be late."

I huffed. "I'll be there."

" A wise choice. And do not even think of contacting that detective friend of yours. We will know, and we will act accordingly."

"Yeah, I got it," I bit out.

"Excellent. I look forward to properly welcoming you to our ranks." The man turned and strode away without another word.

I watched him go, fuming. How had everything gone so wrong so quickly? I'd only gone for pancakes! The only individual I expected to meet while I was out was Mrs. Buttersworth.

I didn't have any idea the Weavers had been watching my every move. That they were waiting for an opportunity to get me alone. That was the only way they had any chance against me. Because they couldn't use their power against me in the open city. I suspected they needed my tree for that. They knew if they had me alone, my family was vulnerable.

A savvy but despicable move. Those clandestine secret society types never play fair.

I looked down at the address again. Then I crumpled the card in my fist.

No matter what this cost me, I would keep my family safe. And when the time came, these bastards would pay.

I needed to get to that address. My phone vibrated. A message from an unknown number. "We're watching you. Do not contact anyone."

Well, for fuck's sake. These people were good. I couldn't make a call. I couldn't even use my maps app to make sure I was heading to the right location. They'd probably suspect I was reaching out to Emilie or Sloane.

I couldn't type out a long message. But maybe I could get away with a few emojis. Just to let Emilie know the shit was hitting the fan.

So I texted Emilie three poops.

It was the only way I could tell her that she *needed* to stay put, not to leave the house under any circumstances. Because *something* was going down. And if things turned to shit—not just the smiling digital kind—she and Merlin needed to be ready.

I knew how Emilie would respond. She'd use her violin. Cast a vision. Find out more about what was going on. She couldn't control what visions her violin produced, but her bardic power always told us *something* important when we needed it the most. Hopefully, she'd uncover exactly what the Weavers were up to.

Worst-case scenario, I could use my staff. I had it tucked neatly in my pocket in miniaturized form. I could teleport back to them. I could fight off these Weavers with everything I've got.

But I also didn't know what these people were capable of. And for now... if the guy in the produce section was at all sincere... all they wanted was to talk.

I wasn't naïve, though. People who only want to talk don't threaten your family. It's not usually the move you make if you're trying to encourage someone to join your team. Unless they knew their offer was a hard sell. They *expected* me to turn them down. They needed leverage. Approaching me when they could isolate my family was their move.

But they weren't the only ones with leverage. That they went to such measures told me that the Weavers were desperate. I could use that to my advantage. Once I learned *exactly* what it was they wanted.

13. Dicks and Daggers

THE SKYSCRAPERS TOWERED ABOVE my truck as I approached the address Alessandro gave me. I reached for my phone, thinking maybe I could call Em and have her listen in. Maybe I could find out if she'd learned more using her violin about what was going on, but another text popped up before I could dial.

Still watching.

Dammit. These creeps were really starting to piss me off. "How the hell are you watching me in my truck?"

We have our methods.

I snorted. "You can hear me too? What the hell?" The Rockwell song "Somebody's Watching Me" started playing in my head, and I found myself humming the tune. My phone buzzed again.

You're not as funny as you think you are.

"Alright, you've crossed a line," I said. "Threatening my family is one thing, but insulting my comedic genius? Now it's personal." No response. Typical.

The address led to a parking garage, because of course it did. I parked my truck, locked it up, and stepped outside. Immediately, a black van pulled up, and three guys in black robes jumped out, grabbed me, and tossed me inside.

My head throbbed where it smacked into the van wall. Before I could protest, one of the men in the van tied my wrists together with zip-ties. "Really, Alessandro? I came here willingly. Was that necessary?"

But when I looked closer at the robes, the symbol was different from the cultists in the park. It wasn't the symbol I'd seen tattooed on Alessandro's wrist. This was two blank twelve-sided dice stuck together, like the kind people use for role-playing games.

For some reason, though, I doubted they'd snagged me for a *D&D* adventure. Though if there were dungeons or dragons involved, it wouldn't be the first time.

"You're not Alessandro," I said. My heart raced. I'd walked into a trap, and now I was in a van with three strangers wearing creepy robes, cut off from any way to call for help.

The van rumbled to life and started moving. I struggled against the ropes binding my wrists, but I couldn't get free. All I could do was brace myself for whatever came next and hope I'd find an opening to escape. The dice-worshippers, whoever they were, clearly had sinister plans, and if I couldn't get away…

Let's just say I really hoped Em was practicing her violin. That she knew people were watching the house and she'd have a plan to get out of there. I knew Alessandro had people watching the house. What about these people? They were clearly some kind of rival sect of Weavers. But what was their agenda? Alessandro hadn't given me much reason to trust him. These people were probably worse.

Maybe Alessanrdo was telling the truth. Perhaps protecting Merlin and his destiny was in their interest. Maybe they really needed my help to… stop *these* people instead.

Whatever the case, there was too much I didn't know to draw any definitive conclusions regarding my predicament.

One of the robed figures lowered his hood, revealing a face painted with strange symbols and markings. His eyes were dark, filled with an inky magic, and his smile revealed a mouthful of gold teeth.

"Who the hell are you?," I asked.

He kicked me hard in the face. Pain exploded through my nose and cheek. Blood trickled down my lips.

I huffed. "Alright, so you're Dick. That's what I'll call you. No reason to get violent, Dick."

Dick didn't respond.

The others rummaged through my pockets, finding my staff. They'd stripped me of my only means of defense. I struggled against the zip-ties again, but it was useless. I was well and truly screwed.

"Just in case you get any funny ideas," the leader said, tapping the staff against his palm.

"Who are you?" I demanded. "What do you want? Where's Alessandro?"

The leader laughed. "We were keen to grab you before he did. We can't have his organization interfering with our goals."

I snorted. "Let me guess. You're going to pitch that I join you guys instead? I don't know about all you Weaver types, but your recruitment programs suck ass."

"We have no intention of recruiting you," the leader said. "You're merely... an inconvenience. But once we have what we want, you'll no longer be a problem."

My blood ran cold. "What *do* you want?"

The leader's grin widened. "The boy, of course. We know who he will become. We know how powerful he'll be. If we can just teach him our methods... well... let's just say this entire world you think you're protecting might look very different once *our* Merlin returns to Camelot."

I tilted my head. "Change one thing in history. Infect the famous Merlin without whom Arthur and his round table would never establish the kingdom..."

"And if the Great British empire never becomes what it did, if Merlin helps us put *our* people in place instead... let's just say the orders of power today will not be anything like *this*."

I shook my head. "Merlin would never help you. He might be young, but he's not naïve. He knows right from wrong."

"But he doesn't yet know who he is *supposed* to be, does he? How easy it will be to manipulate the boy ignorant of his own destiny."

I gritted my teeth. "You stay away from my son. I'm warning you. Mess with my family and I'll kill every last one of you."

The leader smirked. "Good luck with that."

BANG!

The explosion rocked the van, sending Dick slamming against the side. Gravity shifted violently as I slammed against metal and wood, pain exploding through my body. But I gritted my teeth and summoned a shield of magic around myself. It was the best I could do without my staff. I could only hope it would be enough. The van continued to roll and roll, my body bouncing off every surface, but the shield held.

When the van finally came to a stop, I blinked away stars and shadows swimming in my vision. The leader and his goons were sprawled and groaning.

The back doors of the van burst open. Sunlight streamed in, blinding me for a moment.

A familiar voice boomed, "Elijah! Are you alright?"

I squinted against the light, making out a familiar figure. "Alessandro? What are you doing here?"

"Saving your ass, it seems." He reached around me and cut the zip-ties binding my wrists.

I took Alessandro's hand and climbed from the wreckage. "Thank God you showed. These people... they want Merlin."

Alessandro nodded. "I didn't realize they were so close. Our people are good. You've probably noticed that already. But these men... for them to be a step ahead of us..."

"Hold on." I grabbed my staff back from one of the men who was not unconscious laying on the wall of the van that had become our floor. "Going to need this."

Adrenaline was still surging. When it wore off, I'd have a few minor injuries that would hurt a lot more than they did at the moment.

"Hurry," Alessandro said. "These men won't be down for long."

"Then let's finish them off!" I insisted. "Look, they want Merlin. I can't let them—"

Alessandro sighed. "You can't kill men who are already dead, Mr. Wadsworth."

14. ReesesPiscis

The overturned van's doors flung open as Alessandro and I stepped out into the moonlit city streets. The dark-robed cultists inside were splayed across the seats, eyes glassy and limbs limp—dead, or so it seemed.

"What did you mean they're *already* dead?" I asked, one eyebrow raised skeptically.

Alessandro waved a dismissive hand. "It's a long story. This isn't the time or place for explanations."

I shrugged. "Well I want answers. Looks like we're fine for now because—ding dong!"

He frowned. "Ding dong?"

"Ding dong, the Dick is dead!" I quipped. At his blank look, I added, "Their leader wouldn't give me his name. I thought he looked like a Richard."

Alessandro pinched the bridge of his nose. "The man's name is not Richard. But you likely know it already."

My eyes narrowed. What wasn't he telling me? I stepped closer, crowding a little too close to Alessandro as he hurried down the street away from the wreckage.

"No time for games," I growled and grabbed Alessandro's arm. "You clearly had complex plans in place to bring me here. Plans these ass wipes foiled. Now talk."

Alessandro's lips pressed into a thin line. "I already told you. There's no time for explanations. I must bring you to my order's headquarters. All will be revealed there."

Alessandro tried to pull his arm from my grip, but I held fast.

"Your order?" I pressed. "You're Weavers, aren't you?"

He let out an exasperated sigh. "Weaver is a broad term for those who utilize sacred geometry to manipulate reality's fabric. I belong to the Adepts of the ."

I blinked in surprise. The Vesica Piscis were like the Knights Templar or Illuminati of the supernatural world. Conspiracy theories abounded in communities of witches, druids, and even vampires, regarding their existence and agenda. No one knew for sure if they even existed—or ever did. Where were they headquartered? What was their agenda? Some people believed they manipulated the supernatural communities like puppet masters, pursuing some kind of master agenda that we'd only learn when it was too late. Others believed they guarded magical secrets that were too dangerous to pass along to the uninitiated—spells that could literally unravel the fabric of creation and spacetime.

I'd always thought they were little more than an urban myth. Something to blame when shit goes down that no one else could explain.

"Any affiliation with Reese's Piscis?" I joked, trying to break the tension. "If so, sign me up!"

Alessandro's stony expression didn't crack. Tough crowd.

After an awkward beat he said, "You're a druid. Can you teleport us back to the parking garage?" He glanced around warily. "We'll need your truck. Too many of my men have been compromised by the Mordredan Weavers."

"Mordred?" I repeated in surprise. "As in the son of King Arthur?"

Alessandro nodded, his expression grim. "The son of Arthur and his half-sister Morgause. I told you he was dead already. The truth is, he's *been* dead since the 6th century."

I shook my head. "Arthur and Mordred died at the end of each other's swords at Camlann."

"Technically, Mordred pierced his father with a spear." Alessandro cleared his throat. "Arthur struck his son with Excalibur."

I sighed. "So we're talking zombies now?"

"No." Alessandro's response was swift. "The truth is far more troubling than that."

I raised an eyebrow. "More troubling than zombies? Clearly you haven't seen The Walking Dead."

Alessandro's patience was wearing thin. "We can discuss this back at headquarters. Right now we need to move before Mordred awakens again."

I decided not to press him further. With a deep breath, I willed my staff to full length. Then I spun it overhead, summoning a swirling green portal that enveloped us both. A familiar tingle spread over my skin as we slipped between realities. A moment later my boots hit pavement next to the truck.

I unlocked the door while Alessandro scanned the parking garage, wary of attackers. But we seemed to be in the clear.

"Alright, where to?" I asked, sliding into the driver's seat.

MERLIN'S MANTLE

Alessandro directed me out of the garage. As we pulled onto the street, I couldn't resist pressing him again.

"So let's recap. I know the Arthurian legends better than most. Comes with the territory when you're raising Merlin."

Alessandro sighed. "Understandable."

"Morgause was Arthur's half-sister. From what I understand, Arthur only learned this *after* she was with child."

"Yes," Alessandro confirmed. "An unfortunate situation, to put it mildly."

"And Morgause was also sister to Morgaine, known to history as Morgan Le Fay."

Alessandro nodded. "The witch had great influence over her nephew. Long before Camlann, she'd concocted a contingency plan in case Mordred fell."

I gripped the wheel, piecing it together. "A plan involving powerful magic, I take it?"

"Magic that could span centuries," Alessandro said gravely. "Binding Mordred's fate to the rise and fall of Merlin himself."

My mind raced with the implications. I'd always feared Morgana's interference with Merlin's destiny. The elder Merlin warned me such might be the case. But I never imagined something like *this* could happen. Morgana's web was far more complex than I'd realized.

I took a moment to process this troubling revelation.

"So Morgana tied Mordred's rebirth to Merlin's powers? Ensuring Mordred would return when Merlin was weakest, unable to stop him?"

Alessandro nodded grimly. "Precisely. She knew Merlin would be vulnerable as a child. Mordred revived the very day your son was born."

My hands tightened on the wheel. "Because two versions of a soul cannot exist in one time," I murmured.

"Correct," Alessandro confirmed. "While Merlin is a boy, his elder self cannot intervene. And now that your son is beginning to come into his power, coming of age, he's susceptible to influence. The way a young adept's power forms in pubescence can set a trajectory that ultimately determines his destiny."

My mind raced ahead. Morgana planned this perfectly. With Merlin a child, only I stood in Mordred's way. That's why Mordred had taken me. He had no use for me or my abilities. He only intended to remove me from Merlin's sphere of influence.

"He planned to kill me, didn't he?"

Alessandro shook his head. "Hard to say. My guess is he hoped to use you as leverage to influence your son. All he needs is for Merlin to accept the Mordredan mark."

"The D&D dice glued together?" I cocked an eyebrow.

"They're not dice," Alessandro explained. "The dodecahedron is among the geometric shapes that correspond with the Platonic Solids. It's the shape that corresponds with the element of ether—the mysterious fifth element of life, of the universe itself. By the way. Turn right."

I flipped my turn signal and made the turn. "My father taught me that Weavers have been involved in a variety of travesties throughout history. The World Wars. The Manhattan Project. Boy bands."

"Boy bands?" Alessandro tilted his head. "I suppose that makes sense. Though I'm not aware of it. Your father wasn't wrong. The Mordredan Weavers have persisted since the days of Camelot. Their agenda was to prepare for Mordred's return. The once-and-future son."

"And they were the ones responsible for all that stuff? Not you guys, the Reese's... whatever?"

"Vesica Piscis," Alessandro said. "Our agenda has always been to protect the order of time and space. Our sigil consists of two spheres. The sphere corresponds with the divine power of creation. Where two spheres intersect creates a Vesica Piscis, an almond-shaped portal. Every convergence, every gateway between worlds, is a variation of this convergence in the Divine mind."

I rubbed my brow. "I'm not sure what to make of any of this."

Alessandro sighed. "I am become death, the destroyer of worlds."

"That sounds familiar. I've heard that before."

"A quote by Oppenheimer. Perhaps you've seen the movie."

I grunted. "I tried. But damn. That thing was three hours long. I couldn't get through it without falling asleep. So I watched Barbie instead."

Alessandro smirked. "You're not the only one. No matter. When Oppenheimer constructed the atomic bomb. What you might not know is that the plutonium core was a perfect sphere. The detonator was a perfect dodecahedron. It is no mistake that the sphere—the primary geometric foundation of our order, the principle of creation itself—and the dodecahedron, the central platonic shape of the Mordredans, united to create such devastation. Rogue members of both orders were involved in the project. This should suffice to illustrate the power of each of our orders, the devastation that might follow from the misuse of our secrets."

"You mean to tell me that this little pissing match between your two orders brought about the nuclear age?"

"More or less," Alessandro sighed. "Our order is not perfect. We've made our mistakes. But we are not like the Mordredans. Their goal has always been to change the entire world by altering history itself. It begins with your son. If they can convince Merlin to assume their mantle, to manipulate the principle of life itself, he'll be a fundamentally different person when he returns to Camelot."

"And the world as we know it today will be something else entirely." I shook my head. "Dick... I mean Mordred. He alluded to that after his guys grabbed me."

"Make no mistake about it. These men care only about power. Establishing a new world order by reshaping the very foundation of western society. That *begins w*ith Camelot. With your son."

Alessandro pointed out another turn ahead. Two more after that. There was one thing that still bothered me. A piece of the puzzle that still made little sense. "I don't understand how all of this connects to what I caught you all doing with my tree in the park. How it's connected to the shadow monsters and the murders."

"Like I said." Alessandro paused for a moment. "Your son *is* at the center of all of this. He must be protected. But the truth of the matter is not what you suspect."

"Explain, then." I was starting to get a little annoyed by all of this. Not just because it involved geometry—and I hate math—but because my son was involved and Alessandro was still withholding important information.

"I already told you. This isn't a truth that can be easily explained. It must be demonstrated. I promise, after we arrive at our headquarters, everything will make sense."

15. Hell or High Water

The dark smoke billowing ahead made my stomach drop.

"Step on it!" Alessandro urged. "That's coming from our headquarters."

I slammed the gas pedal, speeding toward the billowing black clouds engulfing the mansion. We were only a few blocks away from the Airbnb we'd rented. My mind quickly went to Merlin and Emilie.

"My family, they're nearby, I—"

"Your family is *at* our headquarters!" Alessandro shouted. "When the Mordredans took you, I was keen to have my colleagues grab them before the enemy did. I didn't realize *this* would happen... I—"

"Emilie and Merlin are *inside* that?" It wasn't just smoke—it was a dark, swirling energy. The kind that birthed the shadow monsters I'd been fighting.

I swerved onto the gravel driveway, stones pinging under the tires. The old mansion loomed through the haze, windows glowing an eerie red behind the smoke and shadows.

"Are you sure this isn't your people's doing?" I asked Alessandro. "I saw your people at the tree in the park. Then there was an attack. You mean to tell me that these monsters have nothing to do with you and your Adepts?"

"It's not us." His eyes were grave. "This serves the Mordredan agenda."

The smoke seethed and roiled, almost alive. It was like a hundred of the creatures I'd faced had tangled up in a demented game of Twister.

I grabbed my father's sigil stone from my cup holder and slipped it into my jacket pocket. It was too precious to leave behind. And I liked to carry it with me when I was facing something... daunting and dangerous. It gave me a sense of peace in chaos. Like he was *with* me. And given what I was looking at... I needed it.

I leapt from the truck, staff extending in my hand. Time to banish these bastards back to the hell-realm they crawled from.

I drew a deep breath, channeling pure Awen, then swept my staff in an arc. A blast of light sliced through the shadows. The creatures recoiled, wisping into nothingness.

But for every one I dissolved, another reformed. An endless supply.

Stomping my foot in frustration, I spun and grabbed Alessandro by the collar of his suit coat. "Enough lies! The source of these creatures is inside that mansion. Inside *your* headquarters. That tells me something *you have* in there is creating these damned things. And worse, you brought my family into the middle of it!"

I released Alessandro and took a step back, trying to rein in my anger. He straightened his coat with a dignified tug.

"The source is not the Adepts," he said evenly. "I need you to calm down. We need level heads if we're going to prevail and if I tell you what's truly happening here..."

"Spit it out," I demanded. "Or I swear I'll teleport your ass to the center of the earth."

Alessandro shook his head. "It's your son."

I tilted my head. "What do you mean?"

"These creatures are born of Merlin's imagination."

I stared, thunderstruck. "What? That's impossible. He wouldn't..."

"It's not intentional," Alessandro explained. "He doesn't know he's doing it. But it's the truth."

I wanted to hit something. How was I supposed to believe that Merlin was creating these things? If he was, he couldn't control them. How could I believe that? It was like admitting that my ten-year-old boy was responsible for *murder*.

Involuntary manslaughter, at the very least.

It was more than any parent could accept.

"How could my son possibly be creating these things?"

Alessandro nodded, as if expecting my doubt. "Since Merlin is still a child, the magical gateways in this world meant to be guarded by the gatekeeper—who Merlin will one day become—remain unprotected. The future Merlin will traverse time. He'll thwart dozens of threats to this world across every era—except this one."

"Because the older Merlin cannot engage this world so long as he's here as a child. But there was another gatekeeper…"

"And her time was cut short," Alessandro said. I knew he spoke the truth. The *other* gatekeeper was Lilith, my sister. She'd sacrificed herself a decade ago—and even though she could traverse time, her time was finite. That meant *this era* was without a gatekeeper. It's why so much crazy shit was going on wherever these convergences were, where the veil between worlds was thin, all over the world.

Alessandro rested a hand on my shoulder. He meant it to be a comforting gesture. It wasn't.

"The Mordredans have taken advantage, warping the magic leaking into this world and directing it towards Merlin. They're using this... situation... to their advantage."

I shook my head, uncomprehending.

"This magic is primal. The stuff of raw creation, bound also with the sacred pattern of the life force itself. The sphere *and* the dodecahedron."

I shook my head. "Like the atom bomb?"

"But in this case, the two powers are interacting not to detonate an explosive, but to harness your son's imagination. The force is not destructive but creative. The more Merlin's mind interacts with this... power... the closer he'll be to fulfilling the Mordredan agenda. They're edging him, little by little, into accepting their mantle. You posed a threat to the plan. The more you investigated these monsters. That's why they were keen to grab you earlier."

"Because my magic can dispel this power, I can stop the monsters... that means all I need to do..."

"It's too late for that," Alessandro said. "We cannot reach your son so long as these monsters continue to swirl around the mansion. The more they close in around him, the more afraid he becomes. His fear strengthens the monsters more. It's a vicious cycle."

I rubbed my brow. "I don't understand. I'm sorry. This is all too much."

"The energies pouring into this world from the thin veil, like the one beneath your tree in the park, are drawn to human imagination," Alessandro continued gently. "With Merlin's innate potential, the magic is drawn to him more than anyone else. His imagination gives form to the darkness, his lifeforce interacting with the raw form of creation itself. Every fear, every nightmare—his mind gives it life."

"The monsters he's been drawing," I said through gritted teeth. "You're saying he didn't foresee the murders. He...he created the killers?"

Alessandro nodded gravely, his eyes full of sympathy. "I'm afraid so. The magic has allowed his imagination to run wild. He has given life to his worst fears."

I staggered back as if struck "So everything he's imagined... the things he's drawing in his tablet..."

"Has taken form in this world, yes," Alessandro finished. "I am sorry, my friend. Sorrier than I can say."

Rage boiled up inside me, hot and fierce. The Mordredans would pay for this. Manipulating a child— my child—to further their sick agenda. I would make them suffer.

I struggled to rein in my fury, taking a deep breath before speaking again.

"The monster in the Ozarks," I said slowly. "The one that attacked my wife's family. Merlin created that?"

Alessandro nodded. "I'm afraid so. These creatures are drawn to him, seeking out their creator. As his fear grows, he will continue to spawn more of them. They will all come to him, eventually."

I cursed under my breath. Emilie was in that mansion right now, with our frightened, confused son. Surrounded by the nightmares he had inadvertently brought to life. We had to get to them, and fast.

"The more afraid he becomes, the more power he gives these monsters," Alessandro warned. "His fear fuels them. Soon it may be too late to stop their spread."

My hands curled into fists. No one threatened my family. "Surely you have others inside. Other Adepts who know what's going on. People who can help calm him down."

Alessandro shook his head. "That this has progressed to this point already leads me to fear the worst. Your son is inside. I cannot say if there are any other survivors."

I tried to call Emilie again. The call still wouldn't connect. If what Alessandro said was right, we might already be too late. We couldn't afford to wait a second more. "We have to get in there," I growled. "Now."

I stared at the swirling darkness engulfing the mansion, tendrils of inky smoke writhing like living things. An impenetrable barrier between me and my family.

"How do I stop this?" I demanded. "You're the expert here. Tell me how to get through to my son!"

Alessandro's expression was grim. "This chaos springs from both kinds of magic—the Sphere and the Dodecahedron. Neither my Order nor the Mordredans can undo what has been done. And the Mordredans have no intention to stop it apart from coaxing Merlin to take up their mantle in *addition* to ours."

"They want him to take both mantles?" I asked.

Alessandro nodded. "He must still become a gatekeeper. It's the only way he'll learn to traverse the fabric of time. It's how he'll eventually get to Camelot after he comes of age. But with their mantle as well... that's where his story will change. He'll ally himself with Mordred and Morgana, he'll betray Arthur at Camlann. Mordred will assume the throne rather than die on the battlefield. History as we know it will cease to be."

"Will taking your mantle save him now?" I asked.

"For a time. It will sever his connection to the dark power that's birthing these monsters... but..."

"But nothing," I said firmly. "He's stronger than you realize. We need to reach Merlin, give him your mantle now. We save Merlin and find another way to stop the Mordredans."

But Alessandro was already shaking his head. "It is not so simple. The training required to wield our power takes many years. He must accept our mantle, but it won't be enough to stop what's begun" His eyes met mine, grim with determination. "No. The only way is if another takes up the Mordredan mantle in his stead. By working together, a Mordredan and I might both put an end to this nightmare."

I understood then what he meant for me to do. What he was asking of me. I drew in a sharp breath. "Tell me how."

Alessandro hesitated. "The Mordredans will not simply grant their power to any who ask. You'll have to take it."

My jaw tightened with resolve. I would do whatever it took. "Just tell me what I need to do."

Alessandro sighed. "It will not be easy, my friend. Mordred is already dead, after all. He was beheaded after death in the sixth century, but that didn't stop Morgana's power from reviving him in time."

"Then how do we put him in his grave once and for all?" I asked. "Because if that's the only way to take his mantle, come hell or high water, I'll do it."

Alessandro took a deep breath. "I understand why you'd do this. A parent's love knows no limits. But you must be prepared. If you assume the Mordredan mantle you will possess a great power, the power of life itself. It will tempt you beyond measure. It will take all your resolve to resist its influence."

I shook my head. "Doesn't matter. I can handle it. My family needs me. For them, I'd do anything."

Alessandro nodded slowly. "Then listen closely, and I will tell you what must be done... you might be the only person in the world who can do it."

"What do you mean?" I furrowed my brow.

"As a druid, you have a unique connection to the Tree of Life. The Tree of Life is also widely revered in sacred geometry. I believe this holds the secret as to why your magic can dispel these monsters. If only you can refine the raw power you're using... if you can channel the magic into a precise pattern..."

I bit my lip. "What kind of pattern?"

"There is a myth in at least one tradition there is a shape, a sigil, that might contain all of the elements." Alessandro grabbed my arm as if to emphasize his point. "This shape can manifest the full power of the Tree of Life in the world, within a human frame."

"Can you teach it to me?" I asked

"I cannot. The shape was once taught by the Archangel Metatron to Jewish mystics. However, there were ancient druids who also know the secret form. Your specific connection to the Tree of Life, your reverence for trees in general, holds the secret. I cannot tell you how to discern the shape, but if you can discern it and add the shape—sometimes called —to your staff..."

"You think I can use that to defeat Mordred?"

Alessandro pinched his chin. "Perhaps. It is said that Metatron's Cube not only manifests the Tree of Life but also contains the shape of each of the platonic solids. All five elements—including ether, the dodecahedron that fuels Mordred's power."

"So if I can learn this spell, this shape, whatever... it will neutralize Mordred?"

"In theory..." Alessandro pinched his chin. "But mastering a form like that won't be easy. For most it takes years of practice to channel even the simplest forms."

"Look, my son is in there. My wife, too. Their lives are at stake. History as we know it is in the balance. If there's even the slightest chance I can use this spell to stop Mordred... look, I can get to Annwn. I can connect to the Tree of Life. If there's a secret I can learn there..."

"It will not be so simple," Alessandro sighed. "It's one thing to revere the source of one's power and another to master it. You might be able to purchase a samurai's sword off of Ebay. That doesn't make you a samurai. The same is true here. There's only one druid I've ever studied who knew the form..."

"Who?" I asked.

"Your son. But he doesn't know it yet."

I sighed. Of course. "And I can't consult the older Merlin while my son still lives..."

"The question is how did your *son* learn the form to begin with? Perhaps he learned it from his father... most of what the legendary Merlin knew came from you, Mr. Wadsworth."

I stared at Alessandro blankly. "That's not helpful! You're telling me my future son knows a secret that I taught him... but I can't learn it from him! Because I don't know it yet."

"But it gives us hope," Alessandro explained. "Because if Merlin will someday learn the sacred pattern from *you*... it means you have a way to discover it."

"What way?" I shook my head. "We don't have time for this crap!"

But before Alessandro could speak the sound of sirens stole my attention. Damn it. Just what we needed. "Seriously? The cops are coming."

"This changes nothing," Alessandro said. "Because if we do not succeed *now*... the police you're worried about won't even exist, or if they do, they'll serve a Mordredan Empire. We *still* need to help your son. He must accept the mantle of the Vesica Piscis. It will protect him for now. But he'll still be vulnerable to Mordred... because if your son accepts *his* mantle..."

"I get it. I'll deal with Mordred. I'll take his damn mantle. But first we need to get to Merlin. If he's safe, then I can focus on trying to learn this... whatever..."

"But how are we going to get through?" Alessandro asked.

I narrowed my eyes. "My magic dispels these things. It might not be perfect without the spell you said I need to learn. But If I can forge a portal into the mansion, I can bring us to Merlin and Emilie."

"Mr. Wadsworth, your wife... she might not be..."

"She's alive, damn it. She's with Merlin. These monsters are fueled by his subconsciousness right?"

"Yes, but... it's not so cut and dry..."

"If push comes to shove, Merlin won't allow the monsters to hurt Emilie. I have faith in my son."

"It's not a question of what he wants," Alessandro said. "It's an issue of what he *fears*. And if he's afraid for a moment for your wife's life... these monsters will *make* his fear a reality."

I shook my head. "Then I better get in there. I'm going to save them both, right now. With or without your help."

Alessandro relinquished his protest and nodded. "Very well. If you think you can take us inside, then that's what we'll do."

The End of Part Two

INTERLUDES II

Emilie ◆ Sloane ◆ Mordred

I.2.1. Emilie

I laid there in the warmth of the rumpled sheets, the smell of Elijah's musky aftershave still clinging to his pillow. That man. Just yesterday we'd been on the run for our lives, and yet this morning he'd slipped out of bed before dawn to fetch my favorite breakfast. Chocolate chip pancakes. An angel couldn't be sweeter.

A wide yawn cracked my jaw. I stretched, working out the kinks as I sat up. My reflection in the mirror showed a haystack of bedhead and bleary eyes. Attractive. I breathed into my cupped hand. A sniff at my dragon breath made me wince.

Grabbing my toiletry bag, I shuffled to the bathroom. As I squeezed minty paste onto my toothbrush, a chime from my cell made me jump. I glanced at the screen.

A poop emoji. My heart sank. That meant trouble. Elijah was in danger. He couldn't talk freely, but he was letting me know something had gone sideways during his breakfast run.

Keep calm, Emilie. It wasn't the skull... it means he's fine... but something is going down. Be prepared.

I had to get Merlin up and ready. Just in case.

I hurried to Merlin's room and gently shook him awake. He whined and pulled the covers over his head.

"Come on, baby. We need to get dressed."

He peered out from his cocoon, his curly hair a mess. "Whyyy?"

"Your dad texted. We have to get ready in case he needs us."

Merlin sat bolt upright. "Is he okay? What did he say?"

"He's fine," I assured him. "But he sent a poop emoji. Something's up."

"Shit!" Merlin blurted.

My eyes widened. "Excuse me, young man?"

"Uh, I mean shoot!" His cheeks flushed. "The poop emoji's bad, right?"

I sighed. No doubt he'd picked up that language from Elijah. I'd have words with my husband later.

"It just means your dad got distracted by something. But nothing he can't handle. I just want us to be prepared."

Merlin's face clouded with worry. "Are you sure he's okay? I've got a bad feeling…"

"He's going to be just fine," I said firmly, as much to convince myself as him. "Now get dressed while I do the same."

Merlin nodded, but I could tell he was still anxious. I was too, truth be told. But I couldn't let him see that. I had to be strong. For both of us.

I stepped into my bedroom and shut the door, leaning against it for a moment as I tried to slow my racing heart. A poop emoji. Never a good sign. My mind spun with possibilities of what trouble Elijah had run into. But I couldn't spiral. I needed to hold it together.

I took a deep breath and went to the dresser, quickly throwing on jeans, boots, and a button-down shirt. I strapped my dagger to my thigh just in case. As I finished getting ready, my gaze fell on my violin case in the corner.

Playing might give me some insight into what Elijah was facing. It was a part of the plan. If Elijah was ever in trouble, if he sent those emojis, if I played my violin, I might get more insight about what was going on. It would only take a moment. My visions felt like they lasted for hours, sometimes, but in truth only moments passed in the real world.

I lifted the violin to my shoulder and rested my chin on the rest. The familiar weight and position grounded me. I closed my eyes, took a breath, and played.

I let the music flow through me, my bow dancing across the strings. The notes swirled together, weaving images in my mind's eye.

I saw a great battle unfolding on a grassy plain. Two armies clashed in a frenzy of violence. In the center were two warriors locked in mortal combat. The red dragon sigil on a golden breastplate identified one combatant: King Arthur. The other? It must've been his son, Mordred.

I know the legends well. It came with the territory of being Merlin's mother. I read as many versions of the King Arthur tales as I could get my hands on.

This was the battle at Camlann. I knew how it ended… and I was about to witness it firsthand.

Arthur's sword Excalibur gleamed as he swung it in sweeping arcs. Mordred deftly parried each blow with his spear. They traded furious blows, neither gaining advantage.

With a mighty thrust, Arthur ran Mordred through. But as he staggered back, Mordred gathered his remaining strength and drove his spear into Arthur's chest. They collapsed together, their lifeblood mingling on the muddy ground.

The scene shifted. I saw Mordred's body tossed carelessly into a pile of the dead. His head had been severed, likely to be mounted on a pike. A cruel end for the fallen prince. A gesture Arthur never would have allowed...

But the king was dead, too...

An elderly woman in dark robes approached the corpse. No one paid her any mind. But there was something about her that harnessed *my* attention. A dark magic emanating from her exposed fingertips. She was chanting an eerie spell.

"You will one day rise. When the dead king's druid is in his youth, you will rise. And with this, everything will be as it should. You will be king."

Morgana. It had to be. Mordred was her nephew. Necromancy. A resurrection spell of some kind. If I was to believe what I heard, the witch said the spell would be triggered by Merlin's childhood.

...when the king's druid is in his youth...

A chill ran through me at the thought. My bardic visions always spoke to whatever trouble we were facing. I knew what all this meant.

Mordred was back. Somehow, he was involved with these cultists. Was he the one creating these shadow monsters? Whatever the case, Mordred intended to attack Merlin while he was vulnerable... before he could fulfill his destiny in Camelot.

The vision faded, leaving me with a sense of foreboding. I had to get word to Elijah. But when the poop emoji came through, it was best to keep things on the down-low. If he couldn't afford to text me details, there was no telling what was going on. I couldn't put information like this out there where someone else might see it.

I checked my phone, hoping to see a heart. That would mean Elijah was in the clear. On his way back with pancakes.

Nothing yet. I plugged my phone into its charger. The last thing I'd need if Merlin and I had to bail was a dead phone.

I gently placed my violin back in its case, my mind spinning with more questions than answers.

A loud bang startled me from my thoughts. I grabbed my violin case and ran to the living room, heart pounding.

The front door was blasted off its hinges. Several men in red cloaks stormed inside, a familiar sigil scrawled on their chests. It was the same sigil Merlin had drawn… the one Elijah saw in the park.

Cultists.

I raced to grab Merlin, already dressed and downstairs, who cowered behind the couch. "My phone," I panted. "I need to reach your father."

Merlin peeked over the back of the couch, eyes round with terror. "Mom, what's happening?"

The cultists fanned out, knocking over furniture and rifling through our belongings. Their leader strode forward, eyes gleaming under his hood. "The boy. Where is he?"

Merlin trembled beside me. Could the situation get any worse?

An unearthly shriek sounded from the open front doors. Black smoke poured through.

A shadow monster formed from the smoke in the foyer, all scales and claws and teeth. It let out another ear-piercing screech and launched itself at the nearest cultist.

Merlin screamed. I grabbed his hand and ran for the back door as chaos ensued behind us. The creature was tearing the cultists to shreds, buying us time to escape.

We burst out the back door. But just as I thought we'd made it, a man appeared out of nowhere. He grabbed Merlin around the waist, lifting him from his feet.

Before I could react, another pair of arms pulled me back from behind.

I struggled against the man holding me, kicking at the man's shins and clawing at his arms. "Let go of me! Merlin!"

Merlin cried as the cultist dragged him toward the house. I redoubled my efforts, panic rising in my chest. If they took him, I'd never see my son again.

The cultist restraining me grunted. "Stop fighting!"

I went still. The man holding Merlin traced a circle in the air with one hand. He formed a second circle beside it. A shimmering portal opened where the two circles overlapped.

My eyes widened. A portal? Elijah could teleport, but this didn't look like anything at all similar to his magic. "Where the hell are we going?!" I screamed.

"Someplace safe," the cultist holding me insisted. "We aren't here to hurt you! We're here to help! Now if you'd just stop fighting..."

Yeah right...

Merlin struggled against his captor's grip. His eyes found mine, wide and terrified. "Mom!"

I surged forward, but the arms around me tightened like a vice. Pain shot through my ribs. I gasped for air that wouldn't come.

The cultist holding my son stepped into the portal, disappearing out of my sight.

My knees buckled. Merlin, gone. Taken to God only knew where.

"There, there," the man holding me said. "You'll see the boy again. Once we have what we need." His voice dripped with false sympathy.

I blinked back tears, a surge of anger replacing my despair. I clenched my fists. With as much force as I could muster, I raised my heel, catching the cultist between the legs.

The cultist yelped, his voice hitting octaves he probably hadn't reached since puberty. His grip on me loosened. Before the portal could dispel, I dove into it—and heard the cultist who'd grabbed me scream.

The shadow monster got him.

So be it.

I didn't have the kind of ass-kicking magic Elijah did. I didn't have my phone. I'd left my violin back at the house. But at least I was with Merlin...

In whatever realm...

I looked around. It didn't look like a different dimension.

I was in a common room; the light shining through the window suggested it was early morning here, just as it was back at our place. The house was of similar vintage to our Airbnb. Were we really still in St. Louis? Whoever owned this place was well-to-do.

Strange patterns in gold were set on canvas on the surrounding walls. Ornate statues on pedestals decorated the corners of the room.

Through an open door, I heard a shout. It wasn't Merlin. Then there was a scream. That *was* my son.

MERLIN'S MANTLE

I took off running. Another shadow monster loomed in the hallway. It seized the cultist who took Merlin before. My son backpedaled toward me as the monster ripped the man in two—severing his torso from his bottom-half.

Blood sprayed everywhere. I grabbed Merlin, now in tears, and pulled him in close, covering his eyes. "Mommy's got you..."

I spun around, shielding him from the monster. We had nowhere to run. But if this was how everything ended, if this creature wanted my boy... it had to go through me first.

I.2.3. Sloane

I GOT BACK IN my car and cranked the AC. The humidity was a killer today, but the chill wasn't why goosebumps pricked my skin.

Those drawings. I'd spent most of the night poring over them. And I'd found something that piqued my interest.

Merlin's charcoal scrawls were more than the imaginative doodles of an eccentric kid. Each of them contained a strange shape—like a twelve-sided die. It was subtle, a minor feature someone with less of an eye for detail might overlook. But each drawing had the shape in it somewhere. If not in the irises of the monsters, then reflected in their shadows, or in the wisps of the creatures' ichor.

More research revealed that the symbol matched the logo of Regal Son Investments. A small firm that operated in a tall office building downtown and had several other properties around the city. Was it just a coincidence? Probably, but the symbol recurred enough that it warranted further investigation.

I put together a file on the firm. Royal Son was founded, oddly enough, the same year Merlin was born. Probably meant nothing, but I learned a long time ago never to dismiss a coincidence too soon. Given the strangeness of these murders, the supernatural side of it all, it was notable enough to consider. Was there some kind of connection between this investment firm and the Wadsworth boy?

I had a list of all their properties. All of their employees and their board of directors. Strangely enough, the company's president wasn't the same man who appeared in their literature under the same title. Instead, the official name in the articles of incorporation coincided with another man who always stood beside the man who was the face of the company. A strange-looking man, for sure, with markings on his face, gold caps on his teeth.

Not the kind of man you'd usually associate with the corporate world. I couldn't find a damn thing about who this man was, who he *really* was. He used the name of the company's president, Harold Evans. Maybe it meant nothing. Then again, it could be the key to everything. We were dealing with strange secret societies, probably under corporate cover. *This man*, whoever he was, certainly screamed "cult leader" more than "C.E.O."

I'd agreed to share my progress with the Wadsworths. I hoped they'd be able to make something of what I'd discovered. Perhaps they knew who the strange man was, or knew something about the firm that might connect them to the cultists responsible for the murders.

I pulled up to the Wadsworths' rental and immediately noticed the front door hanging off its hinges. My heart raced. I grabbed my gun from the glove compartment and cautiously made my way to the entrance.

Inside was a bloodbath. Three men in red cloaks lay dead and mutilated on the floor. Blood was splattered on the walls, pooling on the hardwood.

Elijah and Emilie were nowhere to be seen. Merlin was also absent.

I should call this in. Get CSU down here to process the scene. But how would I explain what I was doing here in the first place? My investigation would be blown wide open. It would implicate the Wadsworths—and I knew they didn't do this. Someone else did. They weren't suspects. They were victims.

Still, I couldn't just leave three dead bodies lying around *without* reporting it. That was obstruction of justice. If anyone found out I'd been there, and the bodies turned up later, how could I explain myself?

I needed a closer look at the scene. Whatever happened had occurred recently—but I didn't suspect anyone was still on the premises.

Always assume, though, that you're not alone. Expect the worst, hope for the best. With my gun drawn, I made my way through the house. More bodies. More blood. None of them were the Wadsorths. All the victims were dressed in the same red robes.

I had to wonder. If these cultists were creating these creatures, had their own murderous monsters turned against them? Possibly. I didn't know shit about any of this paranormal shit. Where did these creatures come from? Could the cultists really control the beasts? Did they *ever* have control of the monsters, or had they lost control somehow? Was someone else responsible for the monsters, someone we hadn't identified yet? Someone associated with that investment firm. The man with the gold teeth, perhaps.

Too many possibilities, too little evidence to draw any conclusions.

Maybe I'd find something in the house that would provide more clues. If not about who was responsible, then what happened to the Wadsworths? As much as I wanted to solve the crime, their safety was the priority.

I found a phone plugged in. I tried to access it, but I couldn't get past the thumb-print scan. Emilie's violin case was left unlatched on the bed. Like she'd been playing when all hell broke loose.

I found the bedroom where Merlin must've slept. His tablet was open on a desk, his charcoal pencil beside it. On the tablet was a house—not quite *this* one, but similar in architecture. It looked vaguely familiar. Like I'd seen it while patrolling the neighborhood, back when I used to work the beat.

A dark cloud hovered above the house in his drawing. The same twelve-sided die in stained-glass was featured on the front door. Several shadows encircled the house. More monsters? They weren't as defined as the others he drew.

I noticed four numbers on a brass plate on the front of the house. 4564. Something about those numbers jumped out at me. I'd seen them before.

I quickly made my way back to my car and opened my file.

"I knew it!" The house Merlin drew was a property targeted by Royal Son Investments. They didn't own it—but they'd been trying to acquire it. Until just a few weeks ago when it looked like another organization swept in and purchased it out from under them.

It was strange because the other organization wasn't a financial firm. It purported to be an educational society of some kind. Something called "Vesica Piscis," whatever that meant. How could an organization like that outbid an investment firm like Royal Sons for a relatively insignificant residential property in the Central West End? It was one of many mysteries that were piling up surrounding these cases. Given the degrees of weird I'd encountered so far, this was nothing. But it wasn't irrelevant. It was connected—all of it—but I didn't know how.

I was about to head in that direction when I noticed an acrid plume of smoke a few blocks away. Right about where that house was located.

The smoke wasn't merely rising from the house. It moved with purpose, twisting and turning like a living creature.

I had to get there. Because whatever attacked the Wadsworths was *there*... but when I arrived, what could I really do? I was in over my head. All I could hope was that the Wadsworths were out there. That they knew what was happening and were there. Because if we didn't stop this... whatever it was... more people would die.

I.2.4. Mordred

The world spun about me as I opened my eyes, bile rising in my throat. Curses tumbled from my lips, a litany of rage in a dialect from my former life.

"Damn thee, Emrys, and thy cursed father also!" My fist slammed into the side of the van, denting the metal. I blinked, my vision clearing, and glanced down. A jagged length of steel jutted from my chest, ichor oozing around the wound.

With a snarl, I grasped the shrapnel and wrenched it free. The ichor flowed more swiftly now, but the wound was already knitting itself together.

The pain faded, but my fury remained. I turned to the rearview mirror, examining my reflection. My gold-capped teeth flashed in the dim light, a stark contrast to the worn and weathered visage of this second life. The necromancy that returned me from death had not been kind. My youthful beauty was gone, stripped away and left to rot on a pike in Camelot.

Because of my misshapen teeth, I had golden caps. My skin was marked with strange sigils that bound me to Morgana's power. Even now, I could hear her voice whispering in my mind, telling me what to do. Demanding vengeance and promising power.

Power. The word echoed in my thoughts as I met my own gaze. For power, any price was worth paying.

Emrys would kneel before me. The world would tremble at my feet. And once I claimed what was mine by right, once I took my throne... the past would change. The present would reshape itself around my reign.

My birthright would finally be mine. I would be the once-and-immortal king.

Sirens shrieked in the distance, growing louder by the second. The van's wreckage groaned around me as I dragged myself from the overturned vehicle.

The emergency vehicles skidded to a stop, EMTs tumbling out and rushing to my aid. I waved them off with a snarl, but they would not be deterred. Fools. Did they not know who I was? Did they not sense the power coiling beneath my skin, ready to strike?

Their ignorance would cost them dearly.

As an EMT reached for my arm, I seized him by the throat. My fingers squeezed, slick with ichor, and his shriek was cut short. Hot blood spurted over my hands as his throat gave way.

The violence thrilled me. Contrary to what many believed, I did not revel in bloodshed in my former life. I was misunderstood. It was my father who never acknowledged me. Who denied me because of who my mother was... when he learned the truth...

But now... well... things were different. Death had become me well.

The terror in the EMT's eyes, the desperation, the dawning realization that he was already dead—exquisite. Oh, how long I'd waited for this. A decade in this modern world of metal and concrete. I was biding my time. Waiting until young Emrys was to come of age, ready to accept my mantle. It was all I could do to keep my murderous impulses under control. But now it didn't matter. Nothing mattered. Because by day's end, this world would no longer exist. These people, many of them, probably never born.

I drank in the EMT's anguish like the finest wine, savoring each drop.

When the last flicker of life left his eyes, I let the body drop. The other EMTs stared at me, frozen in horror. As they should be. As all the world would be, once I claimed what was mine.

I smiled, baring my golden teeth. "Who's next?"

They fled, scrambling into their vehicles and speeding away with tires screeching. Cowards.

I turned my face to the sky, tilting my head back. The clouds roiled and darkened as I drew power from the Otherworld. My scream shook the heavens, rattling the stars in their firmament. The portal tree was miles from here, but I could feel it respond. Ichor streamed from the massive oak, blasting into the sky like a geyser.

The cracks were forming. Widening. The veil was tearing.

Power surged through me, dark and intoxicating. My limbs lengthened, bones creaking as they reformed into something not quite human. I spread gnarled wings and took flight, soaring toward the park and my destiny.

This world thought it had defeated me. They thought my father had killed me. But I was eternal. Undying. And I would have my revenge on all those who enjoyed the world made in my father's image.

The city stretched before me, skyscrapers like a forest of glass and steel. How fragile their world seemed.

"Let your fear bring you to me, Emrys," I called. "It's only a matter of time. You will accept my mantle or this world will fall to its greatest fears made flesh."

PART III

The Dodecahedron

The Vesica Piscis

16. New World Disorder

The writhing mass of smoke-like creatures encircled the mansion, undulating and twisting as if connected by some malignant hive mind.

The police lights flashed as an unmarked car skidded to a stop behind me. I didn't have time to deal with that. Not with the monsters closing in around my wife and son.

"Elijah! Wait!" I knew Sloane's voice. I should have known she'd be snooping around the neighborhood. I know I'd agreed to keep her in the loop, but the situation hadn't afforded me a chance. Frankly, I hadn't even thought about it. My focus was solely on my family—and on stopping Mordred.

I spun around, panic and frustration warring inside me. "Sloane, I don't have time. Emilie and Merlin are in there. I have to save them."

She nodded, her usually stern features etched with concern. "How can I help?"

"Just trust me, Sloane. Please. Keep the area clear so I can get my family out safely."

Her eyes narrowed, but she gave a sharp nod. I could tell the detective was a take-charge kind of woman. She wasn't used to situations like *this*. She was out of her depth. But given what was happening on the streets, in plain view of anyone who drove by, having *someone,* who had the remotest clue what was happening, working to keep law enforcement out of my hair was an asset I appreciated.

I turned back to the mansion, dread pooling in my gut. This wasn't going to be easy.

Alessandro gripped my arm, redirecting my attention. "Look."

I followed his gaze. A pillar of inky black smoke rose in the distance, originating from the direction of Forest Park. My heart dropped into my shoes.

"Mordred," Alessandro said, his voice grim. "He's opened the portal fully. This is exactly what we were trying to stop when you came upon us in the park before…"

"How is this going to affect Merlin? Does that mean he'll create more of those damned monsters?"

"Wait." Sloane cut in. "Merlin is behind all of this?"

I'd forgotten she was there. I sighed and raked my fingers through my hair. "It's complicated. I promise I'll explain later, but this isn't Merlin's fault. He's not the murderer. I'll explain everything once my family is safe. Suffice it to say, Mordred is behind it all."

Sloane's radio crackled to life, a panicked voice spouting details of an EMT down, throat ripped out. Whoever was on the scanner on the scene. Probably another EMT who'd arrived on the scene.

A calmer voice responded, asking for the location.

It corresponded with the accident; the van that was overturned downtown.

Alessandro's expression darkened and he locked eyes with Sloane. "That will be Mordred. You must warn your people to avoid engaging him at all costs. Bullets won't harm him. Anyone who confronts him *will* die."

Sloane paled, but nodded. "I'll do what I can." She met my gaze, her own belying her worry. "Call me when your family is safe. I'm praying for you."

"Thank you," I said. I never thought having an ally outside of the magical community would be helpful. But in this case, having Sloane on board might just save lives.

With a nod to Alessandro, I spun my staff overhead, summoning the portal. An emerald green vortex of pure Awen. I pulled the portal over both of us.

We only had to go a few feet—a short journey so far as druid portals went. But it was rough. Unseen forces tossed us around, twisting our bodies under the onslaught of dark magic. My stomach roiled, and black spots danced across my vision. Beside me, Alessandro grunted with effort, jaw clenched.

At last we burst through, tumbling to the floor of the foyer in the mansion. The portal snapped shut behind us. My limbs felt weak and rubbery, and I gulped air, trying to settle my stomach.

Alessandro climbed to his feet, dusting off his pants. He extended a hand to help me up. "Well. That was unpleasant."

I snorted. "To say the least." The mansion was eerily silent. "Emilie! Merlin! Are you here?"

I said a silent prayer. I can't say which gods I believed in—but I believed in a universal Divinity. There was a larger principle, an architect, a genius behind everything. If God—or the gods—cared at all, this was the one time in all my life I'd have given anything for them to hear my prayer.

Then I heard it. The voice was like the sweetest melody. "Daddy!"

Merlin. Thank you whoever-you-are who heard my prayer...

I whipped around just in time to see him barreling down the stairs and throwing himself into my arms. Emilie followed close behind, relief etched into her features.

I hugged Merlin tight, blinking back the sting of tears. "It's okay, buddy. I'm here now. Everything's going to be alright."

Emilie wrapped her arms around us both, her warmth and scent enveloping me. In that moment, holding my family close, a profound peace settled over me. We were together again. Against all odds, we'd found each other.

But this wasn't over. We weren't in the clear—far from it.

After a long moment, Alessandro cleared his throat. "We can't leave yet. Not until Merlin accepts his mantle."

Emilie pulled Merlin back, putting herself between our son and Alessandro. "Merlin will do nothing you people demand."

"Honey..." I tried to keep my voice as calm as possible. "This is Alessandro. I think we need to listen to what he has to say. This is what we've always known *must* happen... it's the start of it, anyway."

Merlin peeked around Emilie, meeting Alessandro's gaze. "It's okay, Mom. I've seen this man before. When you played your violin earlier, after you woke me up, some of your magic reached my room with your melody. I saw who I'm supposed to become. Everything started here, just like this..."

Emilie's eyes flew wide. She grasped Merlin's shoulders, searching his face. "You did? All I saw then was... Arthur and Mordred at Camlann."

"I saw that too," Merlin admitted. "But I also saw another future. What would happen if I didn't accept who I'm supposed to be? You didn't just name me after the wizard in those stories. I *am* the Merlin from *The Sword and the Stone*..."

I rested my hand on Merlin's shoulder. "You are. At least, that's who you're going to become."

"But it will still be many years before you'll leave for Camelot," Alessandro said. "But it's important you accept your mantle now, that you might grow into your gifts and one day become a powerful gatekeeper, a master of the Vesica Piscis."

Merlin took a deep breath, his small chest swelling with purpose. "I'm ready to accept my mantle."

Pride and sorrow warred within me. I placed a hand on Merlin's shoulder, giving it a gentle squeeze. Our son was so brave. Braver than any ten-year-old should have to be.

"Will it end this?" Emilie asked, her voice trembling. "Will it stop the monsters?"

Alessandro's expression was grim. "Mordred has shattered the gate in Forest Park. His dark energy is too strong now. Accepting the mantle will protect Merlin, but..." He shook his head. "Now that the... corrupted power of the dodecahedron is unleashed, it will change everything."

I met Emilie's gaze, seeing my own anguish reflected there. She didn't understand what all of that meant. I was just starting to get a handle on all this sacred geometry stuff. It was deep and convoluted. The bottom line was that Mordred was wielding a power he was unfit to handle.

"Mordred is back from the dead, isn't he?" Emilie asked. "I heard Morgana cast her spell over his corpse."

I nodded. "That's exactly what happened. And he wants to pressure Merlin into accepting a second mantle, a power

Morgana corrupted in him. He wants to use it to infect Merlin, to change Merlin's role in Arthur's history."

"But if Merlin accepts *this* mantle... the gatekeeper's mantle..."

"It will not stop Mordred," Alessandro said. "But the power Mordred unleashed will stop forming from his fear. It's Merlin's fears, his imagination, that's giving these monsters that Mordred has unleashed their form."

"And what happens if we can't stop Mordred?" Emilie asked.

Alessandro shook his head. "He's already shattered the gate in Forest Park. More dark power is flooding the world. Merlin attracted it before like a bright light draws in a bug. But once Merlin accepts his mantle, it will find other people's fears to exploit, other patterns to latch onto, and new *kinds* of monsters to make—as diverse in kind as people's phobias, fears, and imaginations."

Merlin tilted his head. "Then perhaps I shouldn't take the mantle. Not yet..."

I kneeled down in front of Merlin. "You're so incredibly brave. But these monsters that are coming after you will only keep coming. And if that happens, well, Mordred wins, too. The only way to do this is to embrace your mantle. I have a plan to stop Mordred."

Merlin touched my cheek with an open palm. "Kick his ass, Dad."

I laughed a little. Emilie shot daggers at me out of her eyes. Yeah, the boy got his potty mouth from me. Mostly. My bad.

I stood up and looked at Alessandro. "Let's do this."

Alessandro nodded, placing his hands on Merlin's shoulders. A glow emanated between them. Merlin's eyes fluttered shut. The surrounding air vibrated with energy.

Outside the mansion, the writhing smoke creatures let out a collective shriek. The sound shook the whole house.

When the light faded, Merlin opened his eyes. They glowed with an inner fire. The Vesica Piscis symbol glowed on his forehead like a third eye.

"It is done," Alessandro said. "Merlin has accepted the mantle."

Merlin looked up at me, his eyes still glowing. "What now, Dad?"

"Now," I said, "we get your mother's violin. And we visit your grandfather."

Alessandro stared at me for a moment. "Your father's memory. Brilliant. He captured his mind for you in that stone you had in your truck. I knew I sensed something unusual about it."

I grabbed the stone from my pocket and allowed my thumb to grace the amber symbol embossed on the surface. "You said there were ancient druids who knew the secret of Metatron's Cube. My father was a druid in the ancient world, before he and my mom came here to our time. An archangel tutored him. Not Metatron, but Michael. I figure if one archangel knew the spell that can contain Mordred's power, why wouldn't another one? My dad is the best chance I have of learning the spell we need."

"And if he doesn't know it?" Alessandro asked. "We'll still need to seek it out another way. It's the only way to stop Mordred."

"That's why Emilie's violin might be necessary," I said. "When we visit my father, we appear in the memory of the ancient grove where he learned druidry as a boy. It's the same place where he studied with Michael. And in the middle of the grove is another seedling from the Tree of Life."

Alessandro patted my shoulder. "Then perhaps we have hope after all."

Emilie nodded. "If Michael ever taught Elijah's father the spell we require, a little bardic intuition will codify his memory into a vision. We'll be able to learn the spell as if the angel taught it to us personally."

17. The Shape of Family

THE MANSION WAS IN ruins. Shadows still lingered in the corners, remnants of the writhing mass of monsters that had infested the place. But they were gone now, banished by the power Merlin had accepted.

Alessandro led us through the debris, his face grim. "All my brothers are dead." His voice was hollow. "I'm the only Adept left."

Guilt twisted in my gut. I'd brought Merlin here, exposing him to the danger that had cost these men their lives. But it would save us all in the end. I clasped Alessandro's shoulder. "Mordred will pay for this. I swear it."

Alessandro's eyes hardened. "See that he does."

We found Sloane pacing outside, arguing with someone on her radio. Probably her superiors. She was clearly getting some push-back about her insistence that the police steer clear of the area. I didn't know how she'd explain it—but I was grateful she tried.

Relief flooded her face when she saw us emerge. "You're okay. Thank God."

"It was Merlin," I said. "He got rid of them."

Sloane's gaze flickered to the mansion. "All of them?"

"Yes." I hesitated. "But the power Mordred was using, it's going to latch onto others now."

Sloane's eyes went wide. "*More* monsters?"

Alessandro nodded grimly. "The dark energy Mordred unleashed will pursue the most vulnerable. Children. The mentally unstable. And it will twist their fears and imaginations into new horrors."

Sloane swore under her breath. "So we'll have a whole new set of problems."

"The creatures Merlin conjured were simply manifestations of his drawings," Alessandro said. "The new threats will be unpredictable. Limited only by the minds they draw from."

My stomach churned as I considered the implications. An entire city full of unwitting ticking time bombs.

Sloane echoed my thoughts. "This is going to be bad."

I ran a hand through my hair, thinking fast. "For now, keep doing your job. Watch for anything strange and try to keep innocent people out of harm's way. I have a plan to stop this, but I need time."

Sloane's expression was dubious. "I'm not the chief of police, Elijah. I can't just make this go away. If calls come in, I can't order the entire department to stand down. I don't have that kind of authority!"

"I know. Just do what you can. That's all any of us can do right now." I forced a smile. "Thank you, Sloane."

The detective shook her head as she walked away, returning to her vehicle. I knew I'd asked too much of her. But if her efforts saved any lives at all while I tried to stop Mordred, it was worth it.

Alessandro released a deep breath. "You know what to do, Mr. Wadsworth. I must remain here, at the Vesica Piscis headquarters. There are secrets of our order to protect, and with my brothers gone, the duty falls to me." His gaze lingered on the mansion, anguish in his eyes. "But call if you require my aid. I will come."

I clasped his shoulder, hoping to offer some small comfort. "Thank you, my friend."

Emilie, Merlin, and I climbed into my truck. Though I could have transported us straight home, magic always took its toll. Right now, conserving my energy was crucial if I meant to stop Mordred. Besides, our Airbnb was only a few blocks away.

As we rolled down the drive, I sighed.

Beside me, Emilie rubbed her temples. The ordeal had taken its toll on her as well. The look in her eyes reflected mine—we had to dig deep, because this was far from over.

As for Merlin, he'd nearly drifted off to sleep in the backseat, the Vesica Piscis sigil on his forehead still glowing, just barely. The imprint would settle into his spirit—and in time, he'd master its secrets.

The drive home was short, and soon we were pulling up in front of our rental house.

The front door hung crooked on its hinges, glass littering the porch.

Airbnb didn't take security deposits. But they'd charge us for any damages. Minor problems, given the greater gravity of what we were facing.

We entered cautiously, Emilie clutching her violin case like a shield. The destruction was worse inside. Blood everywhere. Body parts littering the floors.

Merlin stared at the ruin of our home, eyes huge. Emilie instinctively pulled him close, covering his eyes to spare him from the trauma of all the gore. "It's alright. We're safe now."

He gulped. "Will the bad man come after us again?"

I chose my words carefully. "Mordred is dangerous, but we are going to learn a spell that can stop him."

We all gathered in the master bedroom. It was the only room untouched by the carnage. Emilie retrieved her violin from its case.

I cradled the sigil stone in both hands. Emilie and Merlin each placed a hand over the rock as I willed Awen into it.

The walls of the house melted away, replaced by a circle of standing stones and the leafy branches of an enormous tree. We had arrived in my father's grove.

"Welcome!" Diarmid—my father—stepped from behind the tree, his eyes crinkling with warmth and concern. He enveloped Emilie in an embrace, then ruffled Merlin's curls. "To what do I owe the occasion?"

I swallowed hard, hating to break the news that would wipe the smile from his face. "Mordred lives again. Morgana's spell resurrected him, and now he seeks to corrupt Merlin's destiny."

Diarmid's eyes darkened with anger and sorrow. He crouched before Merlin, gripping his shoulders. "Do not fear, grandson. We will not allow Mordred to twist your fate."

Merlin nodded bravely, though his lower lip trembled. Emilie drew him against her side once more in a fierce, protective hug.

I told my father of Mordred's ether magic and his plans to warp Merlin's mantle. "We must learn Metatron's Cube. It is the only spell that can counter Mordred's evil."

"You know I have not taught you that secret, and I'm not sure I recall the intricacies," my father said with a frown. "But perhaps…" His gaze slid to Emilie. "If she were to play, the knowledge might surface from my memories."

Emilie's eyes lit with purpose. "That's why I'm here. We expected a little bardic inspiration might help illuminate your memories."

"It's our best chance." I gave her an encouraging smile. To my father, I said, "We're ready when you are."

Diarmid nodded and closed his eyes, settling into a meditative trance. Emilie lifted her violin and played. The notes hung in the air, shimmering with magic.

The pink streams of bardic magic flowed from Emilie's instrument, surging with each note. The magic connected to the stones encircling my father's sanctuary. Since this was where the archangel, Michael, taught my father everything he knew, it was no surprise when a tall olive-skinned man—the angel—appeared beside a much younger version of Dad.

Diarmid was just a boy—no older than Merlin—when he first met Michael. This must've been an early lesson, because my father's voice still hadn't changed.

My father's adult form was a projection as well. With the memory codifying in front of us, he disappeared from view, leaving only his younger self and the angel.

Michael gazed down at young Diarmid with a twinkle in his deep, ancient eyes. "Now, my young friend, I have a secret to share with you. Something you may never use yourself, but one day, you will teach your son."

Diarmid's eyes widened with curiosity. "I'm just a kid! I'm not thinking about having babies! Because, to have babies... well... I know how that works."

Michael laughed. "You have a long life still ahead, dear boy. Someday you will have a son."

"Look, mister. I know how people make babies. It involves *girls*. Yuck!"

Michael merely chuckled in response and beckoned for Diarmid to show him his staff.

Diarmid proudly presented his staff, the same staff I'd inherit decades later, but carved with fewer sigils. As I understood it, the staff was hewn from the Tree of Life itself. But my father still had a lot to learn and each spell he learned correlated with a new sigil on the staff. A small, but intricate, carving that helped form pure Awen into a specified purpose.

Michael took a deep breath, his eyes brimming with wisdom as he spoke. "The essence of all creation, my dear Diarmid, hinges on the delicate balance of five primary elements: Air, Water, Fire, Earth, and Ether. Each element holds a unique pattern that resonates throughout the universe. As a druid, it is your destiny to master these elements in all their forms."

He paced around the grove, his presence commanding attention. Diarmid followed close, hanging on to the angel's every word. "But there is one form, crafted by my brother Metatron on the day when the world came into being, that transcends these individual elements. It is known as Metatron's Cube—a pattern that can contain the essence of all five elements within its intricate design. Should any of these elements be perverted or misused, this spell has the power to harmonize them once more."

Merlin's grip on my hand tightened slightly as we listened intently. Emilie's bardic magic pulsed in rhythm with Michael's words, maintaining the vision in front of us so clearly it was as if we were really there.

"Sounds complicated." Diarmid shook his head. "If I'm never going to need the spell, how am I going to teach it to my son someday? Like, you really expect me to remember all of this?"

Michael laughed. "The mind is an incredible vessel. Everything you learn from me is contained therein, and one day, you'll remember—albeit with the aid of your son and his bardic wife."

I couldn't help but laugh. How did Michael know about all of this so long ago? It was as if he'd already seen the future and knew what would happen.

Diarmid shook his head. "This is boring. Just get this over with so we can get back to playing with fire magic. Fire is fun!"

Merlin giggled beside me. "Grandpa was a pyro!"

I winced at the irony of Merlin's remark. It was a fire—albeit one cast by a dark druid—that had killed my parents when I was just a little older than Merlin. But I couldn't let old memories distract from the scene unfolding in front of us.

"Fire is like any of the other elements," Michael explained. "It is as marvelous and life-giving as the blessings it provides, as it can be terrible in its destruction."

Michael waved my father's staff through the air. Several geometric patterns emerged in a glowing golden hue.

"Each element, you can see, has a distinct pattern at the heart of its essence. Each element likewise has its dual. Where the vertices of each shape connect to the center point of the face of the other, each shape can both *manifest* and contain its dual."

Diarmid yawned. "Bor-ing."

"Perhaps," Michael said. "But this lesson will be important in time. You must pay attention that it remains codified in your memory. All the elements are connected. There's a harmony, a balance, in all of creation that it is the druid's sacred duty to protect."

Michael continued to manipulate the shapes he'd formed in mid-air. Each of them filled with their respective element. The dodecahedron—the one I already knew corresponded with ether, or spirit—glowed with a golden light. But then Michael put the forms together to show their connection to the others. Only the element of fire—represented by a three-sided pyramid—was its own dual. The rest mingled with other shapes.

It was water—represented by a complicated shape made from a bunch of triangles fused together into a multi-sided ball—that corresponded with the dodecahedron of ether.

For a moment, Michael glanced in my direction—almost like he knew I was there, like this was what I needed to recall the most.

"Now watch," Michael explained. "Each of these elements is now imprinted on your staff. I've added them to the base, but carved them so small that you will not see them with the naked eye. Rest assured, they're there."

"Alright," Diarmid said. "So what happens next?"

"You must cast each of the elements, linking each shape to its dual, brought together, into a single shape. This shape must then be bound by divinity itself."

Diarmid tilted his head. "Say what?"

Michael started tracing a series of circles in the air. Just like the Vesica Piscis. "It takes sixty-one circles in total, each circle's edge intersecting with the divine center of the next. Together they form what's known as the flower of life, or better, the flower of the universe. If you lay the elements, now contained together, over the flower, you have Metatron's Cube. It's the secret blueprint of existence itself. With this cube, all the elements—including the principle of life, ether—can be brought back into harmony."

"Got it," Diarmid said. "Not really, but I mean, I saw it. That's what you wanted me to do, right?"

Michael laughed. "Indeed. Now listen closely, for this is what your son and grandson must one day do together."

I squeezed Merlin's hand. Apparently, this was something both of us needed to hear.

"From the staff, your son can cast the shapes of each element. All of them together. But your grandson will one day bear a mantle that holds the secret of the Vesica Piscis..."

Diarmid stared at the archangel blankly. This was all over his head. Hell, it was mostly over mine. But I was getting the basics. I needed to call together all the elements—and by these powers combined, I might summon Captain Planet!

Okay, not really. But if you grew up when I did, you know what I'm talking about.

But it was Merlin's barely acquired gift that was most important. It's what would hold everything together. All I could think, though, was that Alessandro said Merlin's gifts would take *time* to mature. Could Merlin do enough, now, to pull this off?

"Have faith," Michael said, almost as if he'd expected *my* doubts. "For there is one element that most men overlook. The element of the universe, of ether. The dodecahedron."

My father rubbed his eyes. It was all he could do to stay awake. Not that I blamed him. I mean, I could barely *say* dodecahedron without getting tongue-twisted. Comprehending the intricacies of all this was a little much, especially for a young boy.

"Water can contain the power of ether temporarily," Michael explained. "As you remember, the shape of water is the dual to the shape of ether."

"Uh huh..."

"But only when all the elements are brought together, and bound in the flower of life, do they achieve true balance and harmony. There will come a time when a man of ill intentions will release pure ether into the world from a primordial realm—it will overwhelm people's spirits, their imaginations will birth horrors never before seen."

Merlin and I exchanged glances. He was speaking to us. This was why we were here.

"Once this happens, the power released will take *time* to contain. Many years of work will be required. It will be the greatest challenge your son will ever face, and it will help your grandson grow into a true master of the sacred forms."

I wasn't sure if this was good news or bad news. Michael was basically telling us that the genie was out of the bottle. The toothpaste had already been squeezed all over the tube and was splattered all over the countertop. What was done was done. But we *could* prevent the problem from getting any worse. We could use these forms—most of them, apparently, already contained in my staff. The other, a gift Merlin had only *just* accepted.

"When these are cast together, and put together into Metatron's Cube, the ether released can be brought into balance. The cube itself can heal the rift between worlds. It will send the vile one who should never have returned, back to where he belongs."

Translation: this cube could close the portal in Forest Park and kill Mordred... again. At least, that's what I gathered from what Michael was saying.

I glanced at Merlin. "Did you understand all of that?"

Merlin chuckled. "Easy peasy, Dad. It's just shapes. Shapes are so... Kindergarten! We've got this!"

Michael looked up at me, then at Merlin. He smiled *at* us. I swear, it was kind of creepy knowing that an archangel who'd taught my father his powers thousands of years ago in an ancient grove saw so far into the future, into the depths of my father's memory as it replayed itself in my sigil stone, that he knew exactly where we were standing.

At the same time, though, it was comforting. If an archangel foresaw all of this, if he'd set a plan into motion ages ago meant to stop Mordred now, it had to work. We couldn't fail. Or could we? All I knew was that when this was over, life would never be the same. We had a long journey ahead. But for now, we *could* stop Mordred. We could protect Merlin's destiny. And this wasn't something I could do alone. It was a family affair.

18. A Child's Faith

The room spun as the vision released us. I blinked, steadying myself against the dresser as the familiar surroundings of our Airbnb bedroom came into focus. Emilie swayed on the edge of the bed, shaking her head like she was trying to jar something loose.

"Well," she said. "That was... something."

Something was right. The angel's visit had flipped our world upside down. Merlin had to help us defeat Mordred? A kid who still sometimes wet the bed when he had nightmares? I loved the boy more than life itself. I knew he was destined for great things. But he was ten...

Merlin hopped up onto the edge of the bed. "The angel told us we're supposed to seal up Mordred's portal today. That means I get to help! I get to use my new super powers!" He waved his hands dramatically.

I exchanged a look with Emilie. We'd kept the truth about Merlin's future destiny a secret to give him a normal childhood. Now fate had other plans. But letting our son anywhere near Mordred went against every protective instinct I had.

Emilie spoke gently. "Sweetie, we know you want to help, but this is very dangerous magic. Your dad and I need to keep you safe."

Merlin's expression hardened. "But I'm supposed to do great things. That's what you guys always tell me. Well, this is it! I won't hide while you and Dad risk your lives." He crossed his arms. "I'm supposed to be part of this. The angel said so."

Damn. The kid had a point. As much as I hated it, destiny wasn't giving us a choice. This was Merlin's trial by fire, ready or not. But that didn't mean I had to like it.

Emilie met my eyes, fear and resignation mingling in her face. We'd sworn we'd let nothing happen to our son. Now we had to trust fate and a mysterious angel—whose words only came to us through the memories of my dead father—that he'd emerge unscathed.

Parenting is hard. Doubly hard when your boy has magic powers *and* a destiny that would lay a foundation for the entire world as we knew it.

Merlin was right. We had to do this together as a family. I clapped a hand on his shoulder. "You're growing up fast, kiddo. Just promise me you'll be careful and stick close today."

Merlin grinned, hugging me tight. "I've got this Dad. And I know you won't let anything hurt me."

I ruffled Merlin's hair, marveling at his courage. He had more faith than I did.

"So how are we going to do this?" Emilie asked. "Merlin's might have his mantle, but casting the Vesica Piscis takes years of training. Alessandro told us it would take most of his adolescence to master his new abilities."

"We'll go see Alessandro," I said. "Hopefully, he can teach Merlin how to do it. We really don't have any other choice."

I hated involving the enigmatic Weaver further, especially since he'd just lost all of his colleagues. He was in shock—in mourning. But he was strong, and he knew what we were facing. Alessandro knew more about Merlin's powers than he let on. And his knowledge could make all the difference. If we didn't seal the portal, it would mean the end of the world. Either by giving Merlin no other choice than to accept Mordred's mantle, or by infecting the world with *everyone's* worst fears manifesting as reality.

The possibilities, the ways the world could end, with just a few people fearing the worst…

Every conspiracy theory out there would become true. Every nightmare would manifest. Every way that the world could possibly end—an asteroid from space, a worldwide pandemic, an alien invasion, a nuclear holocaust. All of them could happen, and probably would simultaneously, if we didn't stop this.

And even after we stopped this, there was a chance that whatever dark magic Mordred released already could do the same. But Merlin had faith in the angel's words. I had to believe that somehow, someway, we'd rise to the occasion.

I gripped the steering wheel tight as we drove back to Alessandro's headquarters. Merlin was in the backseat, humming along to the radio, calm as could be. Meanwhile, my knuckles were white.

We pulled into the gravel driveway, the crunch of stones under tires setting my teeth on edge. I took a deep breath.

"Ready, buddy?" I asked Merlin, meeting his eyes in the rearview mirror.

He nodded, eyes bright. "Let's do this."

Inside, we found Alessandro digging through a pile of ancient texts, dozens of artifacts all piled on a table. He looked up, surprise flickering across his face.

"I take it you learned what you must do?" He asked.

"Yes, but we need your help," I told him. I explained our plan to use the flower of life sigil, but that Merlin would need guidance to cast it properly.

Alessandro's expression turned grim. "That is no simple magic, even for one as gifted as Merlin. It could take years to master."

"We don't have years," I said bluntly. "Can you teach him enough to make it work?"

Alessandro was silent for a long moment. Finally, he nodded.

"I cannot cast it alone. It usually requires many Adepts. I know how it's done, however. Together, with Merlin's innate ability and my knowledge, perhaps it can be done."

"Thank you, Alessandro. We're grateful for any help you can provide."

He inclined his head in acknowledgement. Before we left, he handed me a large manila envelope.

"What's this?" I asked, turning it over in my hands.

"Hopefully just a precaution," he said cryptically. "But as the last of my order, it is my duty to pass this on. Keep it safe."

I tucked the envelope under my arm. I knew little about Alessandro's organization, but I understood his fear. Secret societies like this one guarded ancient truths and secrets. That he was trusting us to hold them, in a worst-case scenario sort of situation, was an honor.

"Don't worry," I said confidently. "We'll stop Mordred and end this. Once it's over, you can start rebuilding your order."

Alessandro nodded, but his expression was grave. "Reaching Mordred will not be easy. And remember—his goal is to force Merlin's hand. He will stop at nothing to make that happen."

I glanced at Merlin, who was listening intently. He looked nervous, but determined. I put a hand on his shoulder.

"No matter what happens, stay strong," I told him. "It doesn't matter how bad it gets. You can't give Mordred what he wants."

Merlin lifted his chin. "I won't. I know how important this is."

I smiled, pride swelling in my chest. My son had more courage than most men three times his age. Still, I had to be sure he understood the stakes.

"Even if something happens to your mother or me, you can't give in," I said seriously. "Too much depends on this."

Merlin nodded. "I know. Don't be so scared, Dad. The angel said we still have work to do together. We'll get through this."

His faith shamed my own doubts. I ruffled his hair, wishing I shared his certainty that we'd come through this intact. But the angel's words had been cryptic at best.

We piled into my truck, Alessandro joining us, and set off toward Forest Park. The dark pillar of magic was still pouring into the sky, churning what looked like storm clouds. But these weren't normal thunderheads—they were nightmares made manifest. If we didn't stop Mordred and seal that portal, there was no telling what fresh hell might spew forth.

Merlin peered out the window, eyes round. I wouldn't have blamed him if he was frightened, but it was almost as if he knew he couldn't let his fear manifest again. Like those shadow monsters had already drained the last of his fears from him, and now he could face anything.

"Once we get there, stay close to me," I said. "Don't go running off on your own, no matter what you see or hear."

Merlin nodded. "Duh. We have to cast this cube thingy together!"

"And if anything tries to get inside your head, ignore it," I added. "Mordred will use any trick he can to undermine you."

"I know, Dad." Merlin sighed. "You don't have to keep reminding me."

He was right, of course. I was hovering, and it wouldn't do any good. Merlin knew what was at stake here, maybe even better than I did. Could we cast this complicated spell—Metatron's Cube? Would it really stop Mordred and seal the gateway? Merlin didn't have any doubt at all. He had faith where I had only determination. Perhaps, with a little luck, that would be enough.

19. Geometry Sucks

The fading light cast long shadows across the cracked asphalt as we sped toward Forest Park. Emilie fiddled with the radio dial next to me. The normalcy of it all felt strange given what we were hurtling toward.

In the backseat, Alessandro's voice drifted up over the roar of the engine. "It's all about the circles, Merlin. Perfect divine circles intersecting at just the right points. To draw a circle freehand is nearly impossible—only someone truly connected to the source can manage it."

I glanced in the rear-view mirror. Merlin's brow was furrowed in concentration, his over-sized sketchpad propped on his knees. The actual spell couldn't happen with charcoal on paper, but it was a way to practice the pattern without casting the actual spell.

Alessandro leaned over his shoulder, gesturing at Merlin's "Big Chief" tablet as he helped Merlin learn the pattern.

"How many circles again?" Merlin asked, chewing on the end of his pencil.

"Sixty-one," Alessandro answered patiently. "Each one precisely placed. It's no easy feat, but I have faith you'll get the hang of it. Once the pattern is second-nature, which frankly, can only be accomplished by repetition, you'll be able to cast it with a single flourish of the hand."

I felt a swell of pride for my son. He was taking to these lessons far quicker than I ever could have hoped.

If only he had the same focus when we tried to teach him his multiplication tables. Or how to diagram a sentence.

Merlin was a chip off the old block. I didn't give two shits about sentence diagrams either. Relevance had a way of harnessing my attention.

Regular geometry might not be so intriguing. You can only do so much to make words like "circumference" and "hypotenuse" interesting.

Sacred geometry was different. I didn't know if mastery required mathematical formulas or not, but the actual *power* behind the shapes harnessed my son's attention in a way that sine, cosine, and tangent never could. *SOHCAHTOA* be damned.

The destiny weighing on Merlin's small shoulders was immense, but with Alessandro's guidance, perhaps he could bear it.

Emilie's panicked shout shattered my moment of reflection. "Elijah, look out!"

A writhing black mass appeared in the road ahead, featureless except for glowing red eyes. I yanked the wheel hard. Tires screeched as we swerved, just narrowly avoiding the thing. It let out an unearthly shriek as it dissolved into wisps of shadow.

"What the hell was that?" Emilie gasped.

Alessandro's voice was grim. "The darkness is already stirring. It's forming from people's fears. There's no telling who produced that particular... entity. As we get closer to the park, to Mordred, it will only get worse."

I gritted my teeth and focused on the road. The truck's headlights cut through the gathering gloom as we sped toward our destination. It wasn't common fog that filled the air. It was that damned otherworldly magic that Mordred released from the gateway—just looking for someone's "fears" to latch on to so it could take a more horrifying form.

"Let's see your progress, Merlin," Alessandro said gently. I heard the scratch of pencil on paper as Merlin worked.

"How's that?" he asked after a moment.

"Remarkable," Alessandro breathed. "To draw a perfect circle freehand takes most of our Adepts years of practice to master. But each circle is flawless, placed just so. You have a rare gift, my boy."

Merlin giggled, clearly delighted by the praise. "It's easy! I could draw circles all day."

"Could you now? Let's try ten more then. Try not to lose count!"

"Sixty-one! Ten more will put me at thirty-three." The scratching resumed. I felt another swell of emotion—pride in my son's prodigious skills, but also sadness. We'd tried to make his childhood as normal as we could, but prophecy dictated his future. Even as a baby, he'd manifested subtle gifts—just enough that we had to limit his unsupervised contact with other children. He had an uncanny connection to animals—like they heard and responded to his thoughts. Not good when he had a temper-tantrum. If we took away his bottle, a pack of wolves might gather outside ready to avenge his needs, or a flock of birds might charge the window. Plants, likewise, responded to his urges. A tree might bend its limbs to aid him. He once directed a fern in his room to pick up his rattle and drop it in his crib. His abilities only grew from there.

Nothing Merlin did was especially alarming. But it was enough that we had little choice. We had to monitor him constantly—just in case he put himself (or anyone else) in danger.

Can you imagine if another child in his class got on his nerves and a black bear or a venomous snake showed up at recess to avenge him? That's why we homeschooled Merlin. We monitored his interactions with other children closely.

Helicopter parenting had become a habit—by necessity.

I wished we could turn back, retreat to our safe little home in the Ozark woods. But the darkness ahead couldn't be ignored.

Merlin was going to have to become a hero—far sooner than I liked.

The scratching stopped abruptly as something slammed into the truck. The wheel jerked in my hands as I fought to maintain control. Merlin yelped, more surprised than hurt.

"What was that?" Emilie asked sharply.

I risked a glance in the rearview mirror. A writhing mass of shadow clung to the back window, pressing its face against the glass. Empty white eyes met mine for an instant before the truck hit a pothole and dislodged it.

"Another monster. It looked like a freaking ghost," I said through gritted teeth.

Merlin peered out the back window. He shrugged. "I ain't afraid of no ghosts."

I grinned. "Maybe not, Ghostbuster. But many people are."

Alessandro sighed. "All it takes is one person's gravest fear to forge a monster. And given the numbers we're seeing on the streets, this dark power is interacting with a lot more than a single person."

"Ghost's gone now," Merlin said. "But there are more things coming!"

I couldn't look at whatever Merlin saw behind us. More strange creatures converged on the road ahead, illuminated in our headlights. The closer we got to the park, the less smoky and shadow-like they were, the more corporeal and *real* they appeared.

Snakes as thick as tree trunks slithered over the city streets. Spiders skittered about on long, hairy legs. Worst of all was a gaggle of clowns on the shoulder—pallid faces, grinning mouths filled with fangs, axes and knives glinting in their hands.

"Well, that's creepy..." Emilie muttered. She was right. But I couldn't let it get to me. I had to navigate the roads without crashing into these nightmares. Because the last thing I wanted to do, while these horrors appeared all around out of thin air, was to have to make the trek to the park on foot.

Though I knew once we arrived, we'd have no choice. We'd have to fight our way through... who knows what?

Alessandro laid a steadying hand on my shoulder. "Remember, Elijah. The only way to stop this nightmare is to seal the source. We must press on."

I nodded tightly. These creatures might be the manifestation of people's fears, but that didn't mean they weren't real.

The more dark energy that poured into the world, the more the line between imagination and reality blurred. If people could think of it, if they could fear it, it might appear.

The power of creation at work—directed not by Deity, but by terrified and warped human minds.

Just when I thought it couldn't get any worse, a loud roar and a vibration shook the truck. A tyrannosaurus lumbered into view, a black ichor dripping from its jaws.

"Oh, for fuck's sake!" I yelled, craning the wheel to the right, nearly rolling the truck as I narrowly avoided the dinosaur's stomp.

When the truck skidded to a stop, and the dinosaur lumbered away, I glanced back at Emilie. "Sorry."

She laughed. "I think an f-bomb was appropriate in this case. That was a fucking T-Rex!"

"Holy fuck balls!" Merlin blurted out.

"Hey!" Emilie and I said in unison as we snapped around.

A giant grin split Merlin's face. "What? You just said it! Don't be a hypocrite, Mom!"

I shook my head and opened the door. "Emilie, you're driving."

"What are you doing?" Emilie grabbed my arm before I could hop out of the truck.

"We're never going to make it. I need to fight back if we're going to have any chance of getting through."

Emilie slid into the driver's seat without argument. I climbed into the truck bed, gripping my staff as it lengthened in my hands.

Emilie started down the road, driving a little slower than I was before. Probably smart—because if she had to dodge another dinosaur, I'd go flying.

Then again, I *could* shape-shift and fly, anyway. But if I did that, I couldn't cast any *other* magic, and I needed to dispel some of these monsters if we were going to make it to our destination.

More creatures emerged from the shadows. A chimera with the head of a lion, body of a goat, and tail of a serpent. Harpies with the torsos of women and lower bodies of birds, talons outstretched.

"There!" Alessandro pointed toward a cluster of gnomes. Unlike the jolly garden decorations, these were twisted, vile creatures armed with wicked daggers.

Someone out there was a gnomeophobe.

I aimed my staff and shot a blast of Awen, dispelling three with a flash. The others shrieked, revealing needle-sharp teeth, and charged.

Ba-bump.

I nearly lost my footing, but in a battle of truck versus gnome, the truck won. "Holy crap, that worked!" I shouted. "I thought only my magic could kill these bastards."

"The monsters before were forged from Merlin's fears," Alessandro shouted back. "Their resilience matched the mind of their creator. These monsters are forged by common humans, much more vulnerable."

I nodded. At least we knew that conventional methods could hurt these things. I wasn't sure how much that information would help if we ran into that damn T-Rex again. Truck might beat garden gnome. T-rex beats truck every time.

Emilie hit the gas and the truck lurched forward, as I readied my staff for the next who-knows-what that might show up in front of us.

"There!" Alessandro screamed, his voice barely audible through the sliding-glass rear window of my truck.

We were still several blocks from the edge of Forest Park. But there, waiting in a dark cloak, the dodecahedron emblazoned on his chest and golden teeth glinting in the street lights...

Mordred...

I leapt from the truck bed before Emilie had even come to a full stop, staff aimed at the bastard.

"Get back!" I shouted. Blasts of magic erupted from my staff, one after another. The figure stumbled with each hit but remained standing.

Emilie threw open her door, using it as a shield as she peered around the edge. Merlin and Alessandro scrambled out of the backseat. My son's eyes were wide, fixed on the enemy ahead.

With a guttural cry, I unleashed a blast of raw Awen. The figure exploded into wisps of shadow.

I lowered my staff, panting. It wasn't Mordred, after all—just another manifestation of fear throwing us off balance.

But this time it was *my* fear.

Because there was nothing at the moment that terrified me more. I knew what was at stake. If we didn't end this, if we didn't stop him, the world as we knew it was over.

And just like that, a wisp of shadow blew across the street. Three more Mordreds stood there when the dark power cleared. With another gust of wind came more smoke... more Mordreds. Five. Before I knew it, there were ten.

"Your fear, Elijah!" Alessandro shouted. "You must get it under control!"

I clenched my hands on my staff. I took a deep breath as I tried to clear my mind. But I couldn't shake the terror.

As the Modreds multiplied in front of me, what terrified me the most was that any of them *might* be the real thing.

There was only one way to know for sure. I'd have to beat them all. Because only the real Mordred wouldn't die when I struck him with my magic. Somehow, I had to buy Merlin and Alessandro enough time to form the Flower of Life. Only then could we forge Metatron's Cube—the only spell that *might* kill the real Mordred and seal the portal.

20. Shades of Mordred

The park loomed in the distance, shrouded by a black cloud of pure nightmarish magic. The raw stuff of warped creation—ready to turn the worst fears human imaginations could devise into flesh-and-blood monsters.

We didn't just have to get *to* the park. We still had to get through it. We had a mile to go on foot—at the very least. And we were going to have to fight for every inch.

But now, on top of whatever other horrors were closing in around us, we were facing multiplying Mordreds. Whips of smoke drawn from the cloud over the park continued swirling in front of us, the horde growing by the second.

Emilie and the boys fell back, daggers glinting in the unnatural light. I strode forward, calling on the ancient powers of the forest. The ground shook as gnarled roots burst from the ground, entangling false Mordreds and pulling them into the earth.

My staff blazed with green fire as I unleashed volley after volley, obliterating one Mordred after the next.

But it wasn't enough. More horrors formed out of thin-air. More Mordreds and other monsters, twisted manifestations of human dread. Dragon-like beats. Devils incarnate. Politicians—Republicans and Democrats alike—because popular fears of the powers-that-be certainly loomed large.

My heart sank. We'd never make it to the portal. Not with so many monsters in our way.

A high-pitched shriek cut through the din. I whirled to see Emilie drive her dagger into the chest of something like a banshee, silencing the creature.

Merlin and Alessandro were focused—they were still trying to forge the Flower of Life, the foundation for the spell I needed to end this once and for all. If we pulled it off, I didn't know exactly how Metatron's Cube worked. The angel explained nothing beyond the basics. Would it help us stop all these monsters, then kill the *real* Mordred, *and* seal the broken portal in the park?

None of that would matter if these monsters and Mordreds overwhelmed us first.

Tires screeched and a police cruiser skidded to a halt beside us. Sloane leapt out, Glock in hand. She fired at the horde of monsters surrounding us.

"What the hell are you doing here?" I shouted over the din.

"Trying to clear the area!" She popped off a few more shots, dissipating two Mordreds. "It's a war zone out here. My chief doesn't have a damn clue, and I was getting nowhere trying to convince him to evacuate the area. So I came to help."

I had to admit, her timing wasn't bad. We needed all the help we could get. But even with Sloane picking off threats, more emerged from the darkness. They outnumbered us twenty to one.

A winged devil dove at Merlin. Sloane dropped it with a headshot before its claws could find purchase.

"Thanks," I told her. She gave a curt nod and kept firing.

But we both knew her bullets were only a stopgap. This was bigger than anything her sidearm could handle. Even my magic—with the entire forest fighting at our side—wasn't enough. We had to seal that portal—now—or we'd be overrun.

I caught Emilie's eye. She glanced meaningfully at Merlin and Alessandro. The boys were still weaving the Flower of Life, somehow maintaining their focus amidst the chaos.

Once they finished the base spellwork, it would be up to me to unleash the full power of Metatron's Cube. But Merlin was still trying to channel his magic.

He'd already formed three intersecting circles in mid-air. Impressive under most circumstances, given that Merlin only accepted his mantle just hours before.

As we tried to move forward, closer to the park, the shapes Merlin made stayed just ahead, like a mystical canvas floating in mid-air. Alessandro pulled the canvas forward as Merlin slowly traced more circles onto the pattern with a golden light emanating from his fingertips.

But it wasn't enough. We needed sixty-one circles... all perfectly arranged...

This was going to take a while. Even with Alessandro's guidance, Merlin had to take his time. Each circle had to be *perfect*. And we had to keep moving, keep fighting off the monsters to give Merlin and Alessandro the space to work.

Another horde of Mordreds emerged from the magic shroud that enveloped Forest Park, charging toward us.

I swept my staff in an arc, summoning a wall of brambles to block their path. Sloane took aim and fired, one after the next. The real Mordred wouldn't drop so easily. But we were narrowing down the threat—sort of.

Because more appeared faster than we were taking them out.

"We're running out of time!" Alessandro shouted over the din. "The portal's energy is endless. We'll be overwhelmed! Calm your mind, Elijah! Your fear is what's making the Mordreds!"

He was right. I had to let go of my fear. I met Emilie's resolute gaze. She nodded at me, expressing her confidence. This wasn't just a battle for the perimeter of the park. This was a battle in my mind.

"Dad, don't be afraid," Merlin said, glancing up at me briefly as he drew another circle on the ethereal canvas in mid-air, his voice steady despite the surrounding chaos. "Have faith, Dad. We can do this."

I blinked in surprise. Since when did my son become the voice of courage? How did my ten-year-old, who sometimes ran into bed in the middle of the night because he was afraid of nothing at all, suddenly become the pinnacle of courage? I nodded, a swell of pride and determination rising in my chest.

Emilie gave me a small smile. She believed in me. Believed in all of us. And with my family beside me, I knew I could face anything.

"Let's end this," I said. I turned back toward the looming portal, gripping my staff. "Are you ready?"

Merlin didn't hesitate. "Almost, Dad."

Alessandro nodded. "He's doing well. We'll be ready by the time we reach the portal."

I gripped my staff tighter and charged forward, blasting the false Mordreds with renewed vigor. This time, no more shadows rose to replace them. It was working. So long as I could swallow my fear, we could stop them.

With each one I destroyed, I felt a weight lifting from my shoulders. My doubts and fears burned away, leaving only clarity and purpose. Out of the corner of my eye, I saw Merlin sketching out the last details of the Flower of Life, brow furrowed in concentration even as shadows swirled around us.

Soon, only one Mordred remained—the real one. I knew it because my magic bounced off him. Sloane's bullet passed straight through him without effect.

"It's over, Mordred," I called out. "Your army is gone. Close the portal and surrender. It's the only way you'll leave here in one piece."

He let out a chilling laugh. "Over? Oh no, druid. This is only the beginning!"

He raised his arms and more shadows streamed from the portal towards him, solidifying into armored knights with shadowy swords. I set my jaw. It didn't matter how many he summoned, my fear could fuel him no longer.

All we needed to do was fight a little longer... because Merlin was almost done. And once he finished, we could end this once and for all.

I called on the forest itself. Whatever trees remained unaffected by the darkness responded. The Awen flowing from my staff took a lot out of me—all my focus, all my energy. But I dug deep. Because the forest knew what it was fighting for. It knew because my thoughts were connected to my magic, my need, my desire. The trees knew it.

And Sloane was there, too. Her bullets weren't enough to fend off Mordred's army. We needed the Marine Corps to stand a chance. We didn't have that. But we had the forest. The *earth* was on our side.

I glanced back at Emilie. "Let nothing interfere. Fight off anything that gets close."

Emilie twirled her dagger in her hand and nodded back at me. She was the last line of defense should anything get past Sloane and me. Together we weren't much. But we were going to fight like hell until Merlin finished his task.

21. The Shape of War

THE KNIGHTS DESCENDED ON us like a swarm of locusts. I threw up a wall of vines to slow their advance, but they sliced through my barrier with ease.

"Hold them off!" Alessandro shouted over the din. He and Merlin were frantically sketching sigils in the air, weaving together the Flower of Life.

I called on the ancient trees around us, and they came lumbering to life, creaking limbs swatting at our foes. But the knights just kept coming, endless ranks materializing. An army forged by Mordred's demented imagination.

A blade whistled past my ear. I spun, lashing out with a coil of ivy to ensnare the attacking knight. His form flickered, then snapped back into existence, free of the vines.

"We can't keep this up forever!" Emilie cried, her dagger glinting as she encircled Merlin and Alessandro.

We couldn't win, not like this. But we only needed to buy time.

I wove a final barrier of oak, willing to life every acorn in the ground into a living balustrade. My head spun. It took a lot to channel that much Awen at once. The knights battered against it relentlessly. It wouldn't hold forever. We had minutes at most.

I turned to Alessandro. "Hurry!"

I didn't know how much more pure magic I could cast. I knew I needed to save up enough energy to cast Metatron's Cube—once Merlin and Alessandro finished. But I needed to find another way to fight.

So I envisioned a more imposing form. It took a good dose of magic to do it, but not as much as it would to awaken more trees and call even more of the already-active forest to our aid.

My body twisted, swelling as I took on the shape of a grizzly bear. My padded feet thundered against the ground as I charged a line of Mordred's knights. I met them head-on, my claws slicing through spectral armor like paper, sending knights scattering into wisps of shadow.

But more pressed forward to take their place. It was the same problem we faced before. So long as the portal was open, the supply of forces to get in our way was virtually infinite.

I swung my massive paws in wide arcs, roaring defiance. The trees around me creaked ominously, branches lashing out to aid me. Together we held the tide at bay, but only just.

Sloane's pistol cracked out again and again, each shot dissipating a knight.

"I'm running low on ammo here!" she called, her voice tight.

I battered aside another knight, my breath coming in ragged gasps now. My limbs burned with fatigue. We couldn't keep this up much longer.

A pike glanced off my shoulder, drawing a growl of pain. I twisted and savaged the offending knight, but two more were there to take his place. Slowly, relentlessly, they pushed us back.

"Elijah!"

Emilie's panicked shout drew my attention. I saw a shadowy knight slip past Emilie's guard. He was heading straight for Merlin.

With a roar I released my grizzly form and reappeared in all my naked glory—staff in hand. I summoned my magic and blasted the knight apart with pure Awen before he could reach my son.

But in that moment of distraction, another knight got through and plunged his sword into Alessandro's chest.

Everything seemed to slow down around me. I watched in horror as Alessandro crumpled, clutching at the hilt of the sword.

No. No, not now, not when we were so close—

Another blast of Awen. It destroyed the murderous knight. But it was wasn't enough.

I rushed to Alessandro's side, pressing one hand to his wound, calling on my magic to knit his flesh back together. But the wound was too deep, the damage too severe. My power could only slow his bleeding, not stop it entirely.

Alessandro gripped my arm, his face pale. "The spell," he rasped. "We finished it but when the knight attacked, I lost it…"

He broke off, coughing up a thick gob of blood. I gripped his hand tightly. "Tell me," I said. "Is there a way we can finish it?"

A faint, pained smile crossed Alessandro's face. "Merlin…"

My son came over and took Alessandro's hand. "Please don't die!"

Alessando smiled back at my boy. "The magic... you've done it. The form was complete. You must only duplicate it. Remember, with just a flourish..."

His eyes fluttered shut. His chest stilled.

"No!" I shook him desperately. "Alessandro, don't you dare die on us—"

But he was already gone. Around us, the sounds of battle raged on, but for a single, frozen moment, all I could see was the body lying motionless in my arms.

"Dad." Merlin's small hand squeezed my shoulder. "He gave his life for this. We have to finish it."

I swallowed hard, forcing back my grief. Merlin was right. Alessandro had sacrificed everything for this moment. I couldn't let his death be in vain.

"Together," I told Merlin, lifting my staff.

Merlin waved his hands, tracing an intricate pattern Alessandro had shown him. He didn't need to retrace all the circles. He'd already done it once. The spell was now imbedded in his subconscious.

With a burst of golden light, the Flower of Life sprang into being before us.

My staff hummed with power as I gripped the base of it, the place where the sigils were placed in my father's memory. I couldn't see them there, they were too small, but I trusted they were there. Sure enough, the five Platonic solids appeared in mid-air, a triangular pattern filled with fire, a diamond flowing with nothing but air, a cube full of soil, a shape consisting of a bunch of triangles fused into a ball contained water, and finally, the dodecahedron with golden light—the power of life itself.

The shapes moved as if guided by an intelligence I couldn't direct. They bound themselves to Merlin's Flower of Life, latching on to certain points in the shape's structure, then orbiting it like planets around a sun. As they spun faster and faster, they were drawn together into a single, geometric shape.

Metatron's Cube. That had to be it.

A pulse of blinding energy erupted from the Cube, washing over the battlefield. Mordred's army vanished in a cloud of acrid black smoke, their screams echoing for a brief moment before fading into oblivion.

All except one.

Mordred stood alone amidst the destruction, his armor scorched but otherwise unharmed. His eyes glowed with hatred as he turned his gaze on my family. On Emilie.

He screamed in rage and charged straight for us. Before I could react, he grabbed Emilie around the neck, jerking her off her feet.

"Surrender, Merlin," Mordred hissed. "Accept my mantle and join me, or your mother pays the price."

Emilie clawed at Mordred's gauntleted hands. I started forward but Merlin threw out an arm to stop me, never taking his eyes off Mordred.

After a pause that seemed to last forever, Merlin narrowed his eyes. "No."

The single word echoed with power. Merlin thrust out a hand and Metatron's Cube, still hovering in the air beside us, blasted Mordred with a beam of golden light.

Mordred shrieked as the light tore him apart, atom by atom, freeing Emilie to fall into my arms. I caught her just before she hit the ground, clutching her close.

"It's over," I whispered against her hair. "We won."

Emilie nodded against my chest, her whole body trembling. I looked up to see Merlin watching us, an unreadable expression on his young face.

Our victory had come at a cost. But for now, my family was safe and the threat of Mordred was gone. We'd have to close the portal to prevent any other nightmares escaping, but that was a problem for another day.

But just when I exhaled, hoping we had a moment to gather ourselves after Mordred's defeat, a loud thud shook the ground, shattering our momentary peace.

We all turned as one to see the Tyrannosaurus Rex emerge from the treeline.

Emilie gasped and clutched at my shirt. I set my jaw and summoned a protective ward around us and the others.

"How do we stop a freaking dinosaur?" Sloane demanded, eyes huge as she stared up at the enormous predator.

"The same way we stopped everyone else, silly," Merlin said calmly as he stepped out beyond my ward.

With another wave of his hand, Metatron's Cube pulsed again and shot a laser of elemental light at the Tyrannosaurus.

The dinosaur disappeared into a cloud of smoke.

Sloane sighed with relief. All I could do was laugh—and beam with pride. That was *my boy*. Merlin did that!

I ran to him to hug him when Sloane cleared her throat. "I hate to break all this up, but Wadsworth? That little shapeshifting act you did earlier left you without clothes.

If you hadn't just saved the world, I'd arrest you for indecent exposure."

My eyes went wide and my face flushed red with embarrassment. I sheepishly tucked my privates between my legs as Emilie busted up in laughter.

"We still need the cube for one more task," I said. "We need to try and close the portal."

"I've got this Dad," Merlin said. "Why don't you come along… as a bear again. For all our sakes."

The kid was just full of brilliance today, I'll tell you.

Metatron's Cube

Metatron's Cube + The Flower of Life

22. Druid Detective Agency

As a bear, I accompanied Sloane and my family to the portal, watching as Merlin used Metatron's Cube to seal it completely. Cutting it off from any realm. Then we marched around the park, destroying every last monster we found. Did we get them all? Hard to say, but we did what we could.

The archangel's words still haunted me. This was just the beginning. The magic unleashed during Mordred's trans-dimensional coup across space and time would have lingering effects. It could take years before the dark magic that now flowed in the world had done its last.

Until the dark energy manifested, there was no way to find it and eliminate it. Whatever happened next, we'd deal with it.

If that wasn't enough, we had a new mystery to occupy our thoughts. The manila envelope Alessandro had given us before we left for the fight.

We looked at it the second we got back to the truck.

It was a deed to the mansion, the former headquarters of the Adepts of the Vesica Piscis. The deed was in Merlin's name; Emilie and I were named managers of the estate. Until Merlin came of age.

Of course, once Merlin grew up, he had other responsibilities he'd one day have to meet. More than ever, I knew he'd be ready when that day came.

"I don't understand," Emilie said. "There's no way Alessandro drew this up on the spot after the attack on their place. This had to have been done in advance."

I nodded. "It's as if he knew what was going to happen all along."

The entire property was a mystery. There was a reason it was important, why Alessandro needed to ensure that it would fall into our care if anything happened to the adepts.

The house was more than a place for robed cultists to meet and draw funny shapes.

Sloane told us that Royal Sons—the Mordredan investment firm—had also tried to acquire the property at about the same time Alessandro's organization purchased it.

Why had this mansion in the Central West End been so important to both magical orders? What mysteries did these walls hold? I aimed to find out, eventually.

We cleaned up at the Airbnb after we'd finished up at the park. There was only so much we could do. Blood was everywhere. We still had bodies to contend with. I used my portals to send them to the bottom of the ocean. Best burial I could come up with on short notice.

My skills came in handy in a lot of ways. Hiding the bodies was certainly one of them.

Not that we were guilty of doing anything wrong—but I doubted we'd get away scot-free if the owner of our rental found dead people in it after we turned in the keys.

Apart from the bodies, there was blood to clean up. Repairs to be made. I paid for another month and the owner didn't protest—he was out of the country anyway, so we had time.

We rested that night—because we needed it—before we headed over to our *new* house the next day. It was *also* a gruesome mess.

Lots of work to do.

"I suppose you wanted to move to the city anyway," I told Emilie as we stepped into the cold house. "Guess we have a place."

Merlin had already wandered into the nearby parlor, his eyes wide. He ran his fingers over the antique furnishings, curiosity getting the best of him.

"Be careful, sweetie," Emilie called after him. "We don't know what kinds of magical artifacts could be hiding in this old place."

I peered into the library, noting the ceiling-high bookshelves laden with ancient tomes. This room clearly held promise. Perhaps the adepts' records might reveal more about why this location held significance.

My eyes caught on an ornate mirror hung above the fireplace. The glass surface swirled with darkness even in the morning light streaming through the windows. Definitely magical. I didn't dare look into it and say, "Mirror, mirror, on the wall..."

Because I wasn't in the mood to deal with whatever fallout might happen if I did. Maybe the thing came with an instruction manual. But if it did, it was probably in Ugaritic or some shit I couldn't read.

Emilie's melodic voice echoed down the hallway. "Elijah, you should see this!"

I found her in a sitting room, sitting at a grand piano. Her fingers strummed the keys, producing an eerie melody.

"I can feel it... this instrument has power," she whispered. "Like my violin."

I nodded. "We have a lot to learn about this place."

The creaking floorboards heralded Merlin's approach. Our son's eyes shone with excitement. "This is the best house ever! So many good places for hide and seek!"

I chuckled at Merlin's enthusiasm. "Can we stay here a while? Maybe go to the zoo? I don't want to go back to the woods."

I patted Merlin on the back. "I think we'll be here for a few months, at least. Maybe longer. There's a lot we need to do before we settle back into the comforts of the middle of nowhere."

A sharp rap at the front door made us all freeze. I motioned for Emilie and Merlin to stay put as I crept toward the foyer.

Probably just a solicitor. Or a Jehovah's Witness intent on converting the strange cultists who lived next door. But given the Mordredan interest in the place, we couldn't be too careful.

I peered through the narrow side window, then breathed a sigh of relief. The familiar face of Detective Sloane Harding gazed back at me.

I opened the door. "Sloane. This is a surprise."

She gave me a tight smile. Dark circles shadowed her eyes. "Hey Elijah. Got a minute?"

"Of course, come on in." I stepped aside and gestured her through the doorway.

Sloane's shoulders slumped as she entered the parlor. She looked utterly exhausted.

"What's going on?" I asked gently. "You look like you didn't sleep a wink last night."

She ran a hand through her dark hair. "I didn't. The department's been scrambling to cover everything up. Mass hallucinations from a gas leak was the best they could come up with."

I snorted. "That's stupid..."

"Yeah, well, they didn't really want my opinions." Bitterness tinged her voice.

I studied her with concern. "I'm guessing they didn't take your report seriously."

"Worse than that." She stared at the floor. "They put me on mandatory leave. Said I needed time to 'get my head straight' after what I thought I saw. After I tried to steer officers away from a crime scene. They think this 'gas leak' might have been prevented if I hadn't interfered in other officers doing their duty."

Anger flashed through me. "That's outrageous! You're the best detective they have."

Sloane shook her head wearily. "You don't know the other detectives Elijah, but I appreciate you saying it."

"Look, after what you did for us, how your risked your life to help. Plus, you saved the other officers' lives! They'd all be dead, squashed by that T-Rex most likely, if you hadn't intervened. In my book, there's no better cop anywhere."

Sloane shrugged. "Doesn't matter. I'm off the force for now. But I had to warn you—strange things are still happening out there. We didn't resolve everything in that park. I think you and your family may be needed again soon."

I scratched the back of my head. "What kind of strange things?"

Sloane handed me a folder. "I'm not supposed to have these. But I printed off a few strange cases that cropped up overnight. I thought you might want to take a look."

I started to page through the file. There was a *lot* there for one night's worth of strangeness. Many of the sightings were reports of things we'd already dealt with. But not all of them.

Just then, an idea struck.

If I were an animated cartoon, a light bulb would have appeared in mid-air over my head. "How about coming to work for us?" I offered. "We could use someone with your skills for the challenges ahead."

Surprise flickered across her face. She started to laugh, but when her eyes met mine she stopped. "You're serious about this, aren't you?"

"Completely. With the forces we're up against, we need someone who knows police work but also has an open mind about the supernatural."

I could see her hesitating still, so I pressed on. "You saw what we can do—the magic and powers. But we still need someone grounded, who can piece together clues and get to the truth."

At that, her eyes lit up. "So you'd want me investigating the strange cases connected to all this? Trying to figure out what's still going on in the city?"

"Exactly," I said with a smile. "You're perfect for it. And I can pay you out of my own pocket, so you'd be set."

I could see the resolve forming on her face. "Well, when you put it like that..." A grin slowly spread across her face. "I accept. On one condition."

"What's that?" I asked.

"Can I name the place?"

"You want to name this house?" I tilted my head, unclear what she meant.

Sloane rolled her eyes. "No! If we're doing private investigating we'll need a name. We'll need to get licenses—but I can handle all of that. I know people."

"Alright," I laughed. "Well what would you call us?"

"I hereby christen us the 'Druid Detective Agency.' Has a nice ring to it, don't you think?"

I reached out and pumped her hand. "I think it's perfect. Now, why don't you brief me on some of these cases?"

The End of Book One

Continue reading for a preview of Roundtable Nights (Druid Detective Agency, #2)

Book 2 Preview: 1. Messin' With Sasquatch

The phone's shrill ring cut through the quiet of the office, making me jump. I glanced at Emilie in surprise—we hadn't gotten a single call in days.

"Druid Detective Agency, this is Emilie speaking," my wife said, putting the call on speakerphone. "Did you see one of our fliers in Forest Park?"

"No, I saw your post on Instagram," an anxious female voice replied. "I really need your help. The police don't believe me."

Emilie raised her eyebrows at me. A client from Instagram? That was new.

Before she could respond, a self-adulating cheer erupted from the corner. Merlin sat cross-legged on the floor, attention glued to an iPad.

"Merlin!" Emilie exclaimed. "Are you on social media again, without permission?"

"I'm just trying to help the business!" His wide, innocent eyes blinked up at us behind his curly mop.

Emilie shook her head, a smile tugging at her lips. "We'll discuss this later, young man." She turned back to the phone. "Sorry about that. You said the police won't believe you? What seems to be the problem?"

"It's my husband..." The woman's voice grew more frantic with each word. "He was attacked last night in our bed, while we were sleeping, and now he's in a coma at the hospital. The police think I'm crazy, but I know what it was."

Sloane leaned forward, her detective instincts kicking in. "What did the creature look like, exactly?"

"I know it sounds impossible, but it was Bigfoot," the woman confessed.

I raised my eyebrows in skepticism. Bigfoot, really? But with the dark ether Mordred released into our atmosphere, I supposed anything was possible. We had encountered nothing so... material... since the days following Mordred's defeat.

But we'd also been relying on information from a few cases Sloane picked up from the department before the Chief of police forcibly placed her on a leave of absence.

A "mental health" leave was the official excuse he gave her. In truth, the chief knew crazy shit was going down—but Sloane wasn't willing to explain things away, blame the supernatural on gas leaks and hallucinations. She'd helped us stop Mordred—and defeat a bunch of shadowy monsters.

And once you deal with things like that... there's no going back.

So she joined us. We formed the Druid Detective Agency. We solved a few cases and then... we had more crickets than an exterminator.

Most likely, crazy shit was still going down all around us, and we just never heard about it. When people see weird things—like Bigfoot—they don't always talk about it. For good reason. Because only crazy people—or people who eat too much beef jerky—see sasquatch.

That's the popular opinion, anyway. I didn't have a habit of judging people who saw weird things. The "strange" was my specialty as of late. But I had reason to be skeptical about *this* case.

Truth was, Emilie, Merlin, and I had lived in the Ozarks for most of a decade. As a druid, I had a deep connection to the land. I knew what lived there and what didn't.

If this man thought he'd seen Bigfoot in the Ozarks, the better explanation was that he'd seen a hillbilly with a hairy back relieving himself on a tree. And it wasn't necessarily "number one."

"Hmm, interesting," I said, trying to keep my tone neutral. "And you have no idea why this... Bigfoot... would attack your husband specifically?"

The woman hesitated, then said in a small voice, "Well, my husband and the creature have a history..."

I tried and failed to stop myself from rolling my eyes. Dark ether had only been an issue for a few weeks. If these people had a *history* with sasquatch, it wasn't likely our kind of case. More like a case for someone who could write prescriptions.

Before I could blurt out something that would likely betray my skepticism, Sloane butted in. "What kind of history?"

She was taking this seriously. Probably for the best that *one* of us was. But what harm was there investigating further? It wasn't like we were busy. When it came to work, we were beggars, not choosers.

"He's convinced he saw Bigfoot once, years ago, while hiking in Oregon. Then again, recently, in the Ozarks while fishing. He's been spending a lot of time there ever since, trying to track and hunt one down."

I muted the phone and turned to Emilie, eyebrows raised. "Stalking a sasquatch in its natural habitat. What could go wrong there?"

Emilie frowned at me. "This is serious, Elijah."

"I know, I know. But we have to consider the possibility this is some kind of karmic retribution. Maybe Bigfoot got tired of being hunted." I unmuted the phone. "Ma'am, did your husband perhaps provoke the creature? Threaten it or its family?"

"I... I don't know," she said. "He doesn't tell me much about his hunting trips. But you're right, he's obsessed with finding Bigfoot. He wouldn't stop until he had definitive proof it exists. Do you think maybe it attacked him to protect itself, or its territory?"

"If it did, you think Bigfoot *followed* your husband home from one of his hunting trips?"

"I don't know..." the woman sounded exasperated. "I mean, sasquatch migrate. My husband says they do, anyway..."

"Ma'am, have you two watched *Harry and the Hendersons* lately?"

Emilie shot me a death stare. It was a serious question! I mean, if they had, maybe the idea of a sasquatch showing up at their house—aided by the ether in the air that might manifest the worst of their imaginations—was possible. For a man who was already obsessed with Bigfoot—a movie about one moving in with a family might trigger its appearance in his bedroom at night.

Alright. Don't buy that explanation? Sure, I was being a smartass. Probably not the best way to win clients. But I couldn't help myself. Better to be a smartass than a dumbass, I always say.

Sloane stepped forward, tapping her notepad meaningfully. I nodded and handed her the phone. She took it off speaker. She was better equipped for this line of questioning.

As Sloane began gathering details from the distraught woman, I turned to Emilie. "You know, this isn't outside the realm of possibility," I said in a low voice. "This woman's husband clearly has an obsession, the kind that can make someone's imagination run wild. With the dark ether in the air, manifestations like this could become more common."

Emilie nodded, brow furrowed. "If this man's obsession somehow brought a creature to life, how do we stop it? We can't tell him to just set aside his fears. That's worked before, but this man is unconscious."

"That doesn't mean the monster isn't out there. A person's mind can still be at work in a coma. The..." I coughed into my hand "...sasquatch might be out there somewhere hurting people."

Sloane finished writing and looked up. "I've got her contact info and the details of the attack. She'll bring any materials related to her husband's search to our office this afternoon."

Just then, the office phone rang again. What were the chances? Two cases in one day?

"Druid Detective Agency, this is Emilie speaking," she said briskly. "Oh, you found us on Instagram? Great."

She paused, listening, then frowned. "I'm sorry, could you speak up? I'm having trouble understanding you."

Emilie tilted her head, straining to make out the muffled words. "Did you say... your dentist attacked you? In the middle of the night? And then he just disappeared into thin air?"

She blinked in surprise as the person on the other end kept talking. Meanwhile, I scratched my head in confusion. This was a new one.

Emilie mouthed 'set an appointment' at me. I nodded and gave her a thumbs up.

It looked like—for the first time in weeks—we were in for a busy day.

Continue reading Roundtable Nights: https://store.theophilusmonroe.com/products/roundtable-nights

Check out the amazing pre-order bundle offer for books 2-(TBD) and ensure you receive all of the Druid Detective Agency books on release day! https://store.theophilusmonroe.com/products/the-druid-detective-agency-books-2-6

Also By Theophilus Monroe

Gates of Eden Universe

In recommended reading order...

The Druid Legacy
Druid's Dance
Bard's Tale
Ovate's Call
Rise of the Morrigan

The Fomorian Wyrmriders
Wyrmrider Ascending
Wyrmrider Vengeance
Wyrmrider Justice
Wyrmrider Academy (Exclusive to Omnibus Edition)

The Voodoo Legacy
Voodoo Academy
Grim Tidings
Death Rites
Watery Graves
Voodoo Queen

The Legacy of a Vampire Witch
Bloody Hell
Bloody Mad
Bloody Wicked
Bloody Devils
Bloody Gods

The Legend of Nyx
Scared Shiftless
Bat Shift Crazy
No Shift, Sherlock
Shift for Brains
Shift Happens
Shift on a Shingle

The Vilokan Asylum of the Magically and Mentally Deranged
The Curse of Cain
The Mark of Cain
Cain and the Cauldron
Cain's Cobras
Crazy Cain
The Wrath of Cain

The Blood Witch Saga
Voodoo and Vampires
Witches and Wolves
Devils and Dragons
Ghouls and Grimoires
Faeries and Fangs
Monsters and Mambos
Wraiths and Warlocks
Shifters and Shenanigans

The Fury of a Vampire Witch
Bloody Queen
Bloody Underground

Bloody Retribution
Bloody Bastards
Bloody Brilliance
Bloody Merry
Bloody Hearts
Bloody Moon
Bloody Fortune
Bloody Rebels
More to come!

The Druid Detective Agency
Merlin's Mantle
Roundtable Nights
Grail of Power
Midsummer Monsters
Stones and Bones
The Wild Hunt
More to come!

Sebastian Winter
Death to All Monsters
Blood Pact
More to come!

Other Theophilus Monroe Series

Nanoverse

The Elven Prophecy

Chronicles of Zoey Grimm

The Daywalker Chronicles

Go Ask Your Mother

The Hedge Witch Diaries

AS T.R. MAGNUS

Kataklysm
Blightmage
Ember
Radiant
Dreadlord

THEOPHILUS MONROE

Deluge

About the Author

Theophilus Monroe is a fantasy author with a knack for real-life characters whose supernatural experiences speak to the pangs of ordinary life. After earning his Ph.D. in Theology, he decided that academic treatises that no one will read (beyond other academics) was a dull way to spend his life. So, he began using his background in religious studies to create new worlds and forms of magic–informed by religious myths, ancient and modern–that would intrigue readers, inspire imaginations, and speak to real-world problems in fantastical ways.

When Theophilus isn't exploring one of his fantasy lands, he is probably playing with one of his three sons, or pumping iron in his home gym, which is currently located in a 40-foot shipping container.

He makes his online home at www.theophilusmonroe.

com. He loves answering reader questions—feel free to e-mail him at theophilus@theophilusmonroe.com if the mood strikes you!

Made in the USA
Coppell, TX
26 March 2024

30576961R00185